THE SAINT AND THE
FICTION MAKERS

FOREWORD BY ANDREW LANE

THE ADVENTURES OF THE SAINT

THE SAINT AND THE FICTION MAKERS

LESLIE CHARTERIS

SERIES EDITOR: IAN DICKERSON

Text copyright © 2014 Interfund (London) Ltd.
Foreword © 2014 Andrew Lane
Preface © 1968 Leslie Charteris
Publication History and Author Biography © 2014 Ian Dickerson

Published by Thomas & Mercer, Seattle

www.apub.com

ISBN-13: 9781477842997
ISBN-10: 1477842993

Cover design by David Drummond, www.salamanderhill.com

Printed in the United States of America.

PUBLISHER'S NOTE

The text of this book has been preserved from the original edition and includes vocabulary, grammar, style, and punctuation that might differ from modern publishing practices. Every care has been taken to preserve the author's tone and meaning, allowing only minimal changes to punctuation and wording to ensure a fluent experience for modern readers.

FOREWORD TO THE NEW EDITION

The Saint and the Fiction Makers by Leslie Charteris is a work of post-modern fiction. There, I've said it. I think I may be the first person ever to have used the words "Leslie Charteris" and "post-modern fiction" in the same sentence (except for people writing sentences along the lines "Leslie Charteris did not, by any definition, write post-modern fiction"). This is a bold claim, I know, but I can back it up with evidence. Well, at least with an entertaining argument anyway.

I first read the book when I was in my teens. I found it as a paperback copy in my local library—I was working my way through all of Charteris's Saint books, in no particular chronological order, skipping from the 1930s to the 1960s and then back to the 1940s quite happily, and this happened to be the next one that I picked up. The title intrigued me, but not very much more than, say *The Saint and the People* Importers. But when I started to read it . . . ah, then something happened. I realised that I had never read anything quite like it before. It was a work of fiction that was about the process of writing fiction. It was a real book in which the first few pages were actually meant to be a few pages from a fictional book (or at least the description of scenes from a fictional film adaptation of a fictional book). That's enough to make a young wannabee writer think seriously about what fiction really is, about how it mirrors and influences reality, and about the actual process of writing.

I'll come on to the contents of the book itself in a minute, but I want to talk for a while about the author, who isn't Leslie Charteris at all despite the protestations on the front cover of all the various editions. The book is actually a novelisation of a two-part episode of *The Saint* (the TV series starring Roger Moore as Simon Templar) which was first broadcast in 1968. The script for the episode was written by John Kruse, although one might suspect that there were some additions and amendments by the series script editor, Harry W. Junkin. The two-part story was later re-edited into a single movie for broadcast in cinemas. The actual book was then written based on the scripts by another writer named Fleming Lee. There is no subterfuge in any of this—Leslie Charteris wrote a short preface to the book explaining its genesis and also explaining that he was given the manuscript by the publishers, and he spent some time going over it, changing and adding things as he saw fit, to ensure that it had an authentic "Saint" feel to it. So, the book was essentially written by three people—John Kruse, Fleming Lee, and Leslie Charteris, in that order, with possible early inclusions from Harry W. Junkin.

John Kruse, the original creator of the plot, the characters, and the dialogue, was an experienced writer of TV drama whose career lasted for some twenty-five years, between 1955 and 1980. Birth year uncertain (well, not to him, but you know what I mean), he got into TV through working on film sets (he was a cameraman on the 1956 movie *Moby Dick*). During his writing career Kruse wrote for now classic series such as *The Avengers*, *The Persuaders*, *The Professionals*, *Colditz*, and *Shoestring*. He died in 2004, and is probably best remembered now, however, for the large amount of work he did on the Roger Moore series *The Saint* (twelve scripts and one storyline) and the Ian Ogilvy series *Return of the Saint* (nine scripts and two storylines). Before his death in 2004, Kruse also wrote several novels, including the thriller *Red Omega* (1981) which is now available as a Kindle eBook, making it slightly odd, perhaps, that he did not novelise his own scripts for *The Saint*. That job went instead to a writer named Fleming Lee.

Lee was a complete contrast to Kruse. He was born in America (as Fleming Lee Blitch) in 1933. Writing wasn't his main career—he taught English at Washington State University, Miami University of Ohio, Western College for Women, and Florida Atlantic University, and practiced law in Washington, DC (1978–1986) and Florida (1987–2003). As well as seven or so of the later "Saint" novels, he also wrote other books, including the children's books *The Amazing Adventures of Peter Grunt* (1963) and *The Last Dragon* (1964). Lee and Leslie Charteris obviously had a relationship outside Lee's work on the Saint, as Charteris helped Lee with the manuscript of a book he was writing at around about the same time as Lee was working on *The Saint and the Fiction Makers* (*The House on Felicity Street*, 1973). Lee died at the age of seventy-nine in 2012, a committed blogger right to the end.

This complicated authorship for *The Saint and the Fiction Makers* is one of the reasons I would describe it as "post-modern" (the phrase being notoriously difficult to define—apart from the obvious fact that it's "the thing that came after modernism"—but could be summarised as meaning "a creative act that makes a point of acknowledging that it is a creative act"). The Saint novels, probably more than any other series of books, are so closely identified with a particularly individual style of writing that it is strange to think of any of them being joint efforts, or (to put it more boldly) pastiches, even (or especially) if the individual whose particular style of writing is being pastiched has not only approved the process but actually taken part in it. It makes the process look like a production line, but one that is, strangely, turning out individual and hand-crafted items. The other reason, however, is the fact that the book is fiction about the process of fiction. Without giving away too many details, in the plot Simon Templar discovers that an entire criminal gang named SWORD has been set up to duplicate in exact detail a criminal gang in a series of books by writer Amos Klein. The gang leader—an obsessive fan—then kidnaps Templar, thinking that he is Klein, in order that the writer can then create the ultimate heist for him. Amos Klein, however, doesn't exist—it's a pseudonym used by the real writer. So, the Saint (who is really Simon Templar) is mistaken for Amos Klein (who is really the female Amity Little) and forced to write a book that will be turned into reality (thus subverting the usual process where elements of reality are turned into books). And all that from a TV script that was in turn transformed into a book by a small team of writers all adhering to a common style. But let's remember that the Saint series itself made knowing nods to the fact that it was a TV series by having its hero—Simon Templar—turn to the camera and lift a knowing eyebrow at the audience just before the main title sequence. "Breaking the fourth wall," it's called.

It's only on rereading the book that I have come to realise the effect that it had on me as a young reader and nascent writer. I distinctly remember duplicating the opening few pages, which themselves were a pastiche of the James Bond films of the time, and then continuing the "fictional" Amos Klein story onwards as a short story for my English class at school. That led to the best piece of writing advice I have ever been given, from a despairing English teacher: "Andrew, why are the characters doing these things?" As a result of that single question, I started thinking about characterisation and motivation, and I haven't really stopped.

Of course, motivation in *The Saint and the Fiction Makers* is relatively simple. Actress Carol Henley is a fame-obsessed bimbo, producer Paul Starnmeck is in it for the money, Amity Little writes because that's what she does best, while the members of SWORD do what they do purely because they are criminals.

And Simon Templar does what he does because he's the Saint. Of course.

—*Andrew Lane*

THE SAINT AND THE FICTION MAKERS

PREFACE

The history of this book repeats that of *The Saint on TV* and *The Saint Returns*. That is, it started life as a television scenario, not written by me, and not based on anything that I created except the character of Simon Templar. After its second draft, I was allowed to make some suggestions, not all of which were adopted. However, in this readable adaptation by Fleming Lee (who also worked on those other two) I have availed myself of the producer's privilege in reverse: just as movie producers always take unto themselves the right to change any story they have bought in adapting it to the screen, so I, with the collaboration of Fleming Lee, did not hesitate to make what improvements I thought I could see in translating the screen play to the printed page.

The only difference between this and our previous experiments is that *The Fiction Makers* in its original form seemed much too good and spacious an idea to throw away on just one TV show, and was therefore expanded first into a two-parter, and then abducted bodily out of the television series to be presented as a full-length feature film. In conformity with that aggrandizement, this adaptation has become a full-length novel.

As with the preceding composites, I worked closely with Fleming Lee on this adaptation, and personally revised the final manuscript to satisfy myself that it was as close to an authentic Saint book as anything could be of which I had not written every line myself. But the only honest way to present a work like this, to which three other writers have contributed their imagination and their talents in such measure, seems to me to be to give them full credit as co-authors—unprecedented perhaps in the middle world where ghosts walk.

—Leslie Charteris (1968)

CHAPTER ONE:

HOW SIMON TEMPLAR DODGED A PARTY AND LEARNED NEW FACTS ABOUT LITERATURE

1

Like a monstrous silver manta ray, the giant hovercraft moved over the marshy plain. Fleeing ahead of it across the treeless flat-land, Charles Lake's jeep seemed in comparison no larger than a darting minnow.

The chase was as unequal in other factors as in size. Lake had no true road to follow, only a pair of pitted ruts which at intervals almost disappeared entirely or were submerged in mud and water. His only real chance of escape had been to drive out of sight of the hovercraft before its crew had noticed he was gone. Now that they were in pursuit, he could see no hope of outdistancing or evading them. His jeep's speed was reduced by holes and bogs, while the hovercraft roared effortlessly along on its cushion of air two feet above the ground. Propelled at an unvarying seventy miles an hour, it would overtake Lake within a minute.

His jaw set, he glanced anxiously over his shoulder at the huge shape bearing down on him. If he could not escape the machine, he would have to fight it. He slowed a little, allowing the hovercraft to come within fifty yards. Having no braking mechanism, the craft began to slow cautiously by reducing power. It was then that Charles

Lake stamped his jeep's accelerator to the floor and shot ahead in a fresh burst of speed.

Behind him he could hear the sudden change in tone of the hovercraft's propellers as it once more put on full speed. It was almost on him, only sixty or seventy feet behind. At that moment Lake brought his foot down on his brake pedal in a move that brought the jeep to a sudden halt and took the pilot of the hovercraft completely by surprise. With no way of stopping quickly and no way of making a sharp turn at such speed, the machine hurtled helplessly towards the jeep like a flat stone on ice.

Lake, the instant his vehicle had stopped, had rolled from the driver's seat and scrambled for safety. He heard the hovercraft's metal front crash into the jeep, and looked in time to see the pursuing monster swing to one side, its rear jarred high into the air as its front came to an abrupt halt. The fans which held it off the ground, set out of sight within the base of the body, were not designed to make it fly, so the rear, which had been thrown into the air, came down with all the force of its tons of dead weight, overriding the cushioning fans and smashing into the ground. It bounced up again, helped by the still operating fans, while the pilot cut off the upper propellers.

Charles Lake dashed forward at the machine, tearing one of the metal buttons from his jacket. It was much heavier than an ordinary button, and as it was torn from the threads which had held it a pin was released which activated the fuse inside. Lake tossed the button with perfect aim under the hovercraft and himself to the ground with his hands over his head.

The fantastically powerful explosion which followed disabled at least two of the four supporting fans. The hovercraft crunched to the ground, helpless. Even before the shower of mud and stones thrown from beneath the machine had come to earth, Lake ran to the hovercraft and leaped up its sloping side. The thing was as large as an ordinary house. The pilot's cabin was a plastic dome set among the propeller columns on top, and inside that transparent cover Lake could see one man collapsed forward on the control and another on his feet with pistol in hand.

Seeing Lake, who was carrying no weapon, the man threw open the sliding hatch of the plastic dome and fired wildly. Lake dodged, tore another button from his jacket, and sprawled flat on the metal skin of the machine as he threw the miniature bomb past the man with the pistol into the cabin. An instant later the cabin and its former occupants were an unrecognizable smoking wreckage.

Lake leaped inside, kicked open the door which led down into the main deck of the craft, and felled a startled crewman with a karate chop to the throat. Taking the man's pistol, he ran on, sure of his way since he had been in the craft only minutes before, until he came to a door at the end of the deck. It was unlocked, and he flung it open, ready to fire.

"Welcome, Mr Lake. Drop your gun or the girl dies."

The man who spoke, the leader who called himself Warlock, stood with his hand on an electronic control panel. On a steel table, her wrists and ankles clamped firmly to the metal slab, lay Warlock's hostage, beautiful, blonde, almost nude. She could only writhe futilely as a blinding ray of light from the ceiling moved along the slab towards her, melting the steel in a bubbling channel as it came.

Simon Templar's profile was illuminated by the flickering Technicolor glare as he inclined his head to speak to the girl sitting beside him.

"Ten to one that gorgeous form of yours comes through unbarbecued," he whispered.

She was the same girl who was clamped to the steel slab on the screen, and so she seemed eminently well-qualified to appreciate his comment.

Carol Henley's narcissistic engrossment with her own shadow had been almost embarrassingly intense throughout the film, but now she managed to tear her eyes away from her picture long enough to glance at the face of her companion. It was a keenly active, momentarily ironical face whose startlingly handsome swashbuckler's features might have stretched credulity almost as far as the events in the film he had been watching for the past ninety minutes.

"You do look irritatingly relaxed about the whole thing, I must say," the actress whispered back. "Aren't you the least bit worried about what might happen to me?"

"Not in the least," Simon answered with a shrug. "A clever producer like Starnmeck isn't likely to let them kill his highest-paid sex symbol, especially when she's been on the side of the angels since the beginning. That's one of the rewards of virtue and top billing."

When Simon Templar's prediction was almost immediately fulfilled, Carol Henley turned up her lovely nose in feigned exasperation and concentrated on the scene of her rescue, which was effected when Charles Lake caused the chief villain's body to short-circuit an electrical control panel in time to stall the sparkling death ray just before it took its first searing taste of Carol's excitingly exposed flesh. The film ended in a geyser of sparks, a skull-quaking series of stereophonic explosions, and a close-up view of Carol Henley's lips—eight hundred times life size—readying themselves for the attentions of her hero, that same Charles Lake who, as of tonight's premiere, completed his fourth consecutive cinematic fouling-up of the machinations of SWORD— the Secret World Organization for Retribution and Destruction.

The screen dimmed, and the first-night London audience blinked its way back from fantasy as the cinema lights came on, applauding with a vehemence that Simon Templar could only think must reflect the hidden but deeply persistent yearning of modern man for the taste of violence and derring-do.

Of all the people in the cinema, he alone, Simon Templar, could be said to have lived a life which for excitement, danger, and impossible adventure equalled that of the fictional Charles Lake. And yet even the Saint—as Simon Templar was more widely known, feared, and uneasily admired by both the police and the criminal world in his role of modern buccaneer—felt amused and refreshed by his filmic voyage into a land of utter improbability. At the same time he felt, as the other members of the audience must have felt to a much greater extent, a certain let-down at being forced to return to the limitations of the everyday world.

As the Saint stood and moved along the row of seats towards the aisle, only that disturbing hint of piracy in his features would have separated him from the rest of the fashionable crowd. His soberly cut dark suit minimized the trained musculature beneath it, and the sapphire eyes that could sometimes blaze with blue fire or freeze into chips of ice were lazily relaxed. Only those who knew his fantastic history would have believed that in other moods he had been the source of more massive epidemics of insomnia in Scotland Yard and in the haunts of the Ungodly than could have been caused by all the coffee and traffic noise in London combined.

"Wasn't I divine?" Carol Henley exclaimed, in what Simon thought was a commendable burst of candour.

"Magnificent," he said solemnly. "Fortunately Sarah Bernhardt has already gone to her just reward, or you might have hastened her on the way."

When Carol gave him a dubious look he went on:

"The divine Sarah had to at least recite the alphabet to thrill an audience—so they say—but all you have to do is lie there and wiggle without making a sound."

Carol beamed and squeezed his hand as they joined the sluggish human river in the aisles.

"Well, thank you very much, Simon. That's about the nicest thing anybody ever said to me."

The Saint coughed and saw her torn from his grasp by a horde of congratulatory and self-congratulatory assistant directors, technicians, minor actors, and financial backers. Having only just met her that evening, Simon hoped he would be able to retrieve her before long. Meanwhile, being several inches taller than almost everyone else in the cinema, he looked around for other people he might know or recognize.

The producer of the film, Paul Starnmeck, whom Simon had first met at a dinner party several weeks before, and whose invitation was the reason for the Saint's unwonted attendance at a motion-picture premiere, was accepting the homage of toadies in the lobby just outside the auditorium. He was a florid man of substantial bulk, most of it distributed along the horizontal, and it cost him some effort to thrust his way back against the current of the human flood to grasp Simon's hand and peer up questioningly at his face.

Simon knew what the question was, because the producer had explained to him in extending the invitation that while he was primarily eager for the pleasure of the Saint's company, though laughingly not unmindful of a certain extra fillip which would be added to the premiere's publicity by the presence of an almost mythical real-life adventurer, he was also interested in having Simon Templar's opinion of the film. The three previously released adventures of Charles Lake in his war against that apparently omniscient and virtually omnipotent organization SWORD had aroused a public enthusiasm almost unequalled since the introduction of the smoke of burning tobacco leaves into the lungs of European man. But there was always room for improvement, Starnmeck had admitted, and the success of the Charles Lake films had started a flash flood of imitations, each trying to out-exaggerate the other. Maybe the Saint's spontaneous reactions would suggest how to keep the Starnmeck product ahead of the competition.

"Good evening, Mr Starnmeck," Simon said pleasantly but non-committally, in response to the questioning look.

The producer glanced around somewhat guiltily and made a skilful kind of blocking turn of his broad body to cut off his recent entourage and isolate himself with the Saint as much as was possible in the crush.

"It may not be great art," he said tentatively, "but it moves."

"To quote Galileo," agreed the Saint amiably.

"I beg your pardon?"

"To quote Galileo after his trial: 'Nevertheless, it moves.' Of course he was talking about the earth, wasn't he?"

"Of course," producer Starnmeck said blankly.

"But it amounts to the same thing," Simon said, glancing about in hopes that he had not lost Carol Henley entirely. "They both move—the earth and your film. They move predictably, but they move."

"I'm glad you think so," the producer said with uncertain relief.

"Yes," said the Saint. "That's one of the advantages of life, and one of its disadvantages too: predictability. Most people are caught in a web of predictabilities that's both comforting and stifling. People think they want security, but underneath they'd give almost anything to have the nerve to face the unpredictable, or at least the unlikely. So I think you can relax. You may only make a few millions, but it's still money."

"Maybe so," Starnmeck said. "But this is a cut-throat business, Mr Templar. Now, did anything occur to you that might make the next picture better still?"

"Well, have you thought about the Unities prescribed by Aristotle for all tragedy?" Simon suggested, warming to the torment of Starnmeck as he realized that he had indeed lost Carol Henley, possibly forever. "How about them?"

"About what?" Starnmeck asked.

"Aristotle's Unities," repeated the Saint patiently.

Starnmeck had begun to perspire noticeably.

"Maybe we'd better discuss this at the party. It's pretty noisy here."

"Fine," said Simon with a slight bow. "Until then."

The cool mocking of his eyes was in marked contrast to Starnmeck's intense humidity, as the producer turned to submerge himself again in the less confusing comments of his own kind.

Simon started towards the open doors which led to the street, anxious to be out of the press of bodies and the hubbub of voices, but he was not yet destined to escape. In fact, Destiny, intruding itself again in the form of an insistent tug at his sleeve which stopped him before he could complete his escape, had plans for the Saint which were to seem almost as incredible as the film he had just watched.

2

Simon turned, looked down at the long saturnine face, the rapidly blinking black eyes, the perfectly oblong moustache like a strip of furry tape, the damp strands of suspiciously dark hair combed carefully forward over an otherwise vacant dome, and saw that the sleeve-tugger was Finlay Hugoson, the publisher of the Charles Lake books on which the Starnmeck films were based. They had first met that evening at the small and highly exclusive cocktail party, held in a suite at the Dorchester, before the premiere.

"Well, Mr Templar, I suppose Charles Lake's exploits are old hat to a man like yourself."

The Saint shrugged. He found Hugoson likeable enough and admirably lacking the gaudy and blatantly artificial affectations that marred the personalities of so many of the other guests. But after his initial favourable impression, Simon had been put off by the publisher's sudden almost frantic reaction when he realized that the Mr Templar he had been speaking to so chattily was that Robin Hood of modern crime called the Saint. From that moment of realization, Hugoson had lost his casual poise and become nervously inhibited and overly attentive, like a man who had something urgent to say but was afraid to say it. Even when they had been separated to opposite ends of the room, he had felt Hugoson's eyes continually switching back to him. Now, in the lobby of the cinema the publisher gave Simon a premonition that he was going to be much harder to shake off.

"They're no more old hat to me than anybody else," Simon said in response to Hugoson's opening remark. "We all have fantastic dreams. I happen to have a knack for putting mine into practice. Your author has a knack for putting his on paper. It's just that paper leaves quite a bit more freedom than real life."

Hugoson stuck close beside him as the Saint strolled through the rapidly emptying lobby towards the doors which led to the open area under the marquee.

"You weren't bored, then?"

"Not a bit. As a matter of fact, I've read all seven of the books by your Mr Amos Klein, and he has an unabashed disregard for probability and the laws of nature that completely intrigues me. Reading him is the next best thing to floating free in space. And apparently several million other people think so too."

They stepped out into the wide space between the front doors of the theatre and the street, where a milling throng was gathered in a chaos of blinding lights, cameras, microphones, and departing taxicabs and limousines.

"I'm sure Mr Klein would be delighted to hear your opinion of his work," Hugoson said.

"I'd be delighted to tell him," the Saint replied. "Where is he?"

"That's what a lot of people would like to know," the publisher said, not with the morose air of an entrepreneur who has misplaced a valuable property but with the twinkling eyes of a man enjoying a secret.

The Saint arched his brows in mild surprise.

"Don't you know where he is?"

"Mr Klein? Oh, yes. I know where he is, but nobody else does."

"Presumably Mr Klein knows."

The publisher nodded.

"Of course. But otherwise . . ."

Hugoson spread out his hands. Simon paused and looked at the publisher in a lightning storm of popping flashbulbs. He felt that the man was deliberately trying to arouse his curiosity for some more than frivolous reason, and that fact rather than any real interest in the whereabouts of Mr Amos Klein began to arouse his curiosity.

"Shall I guess?" he asked. "You have him locked in a hen coop at the bottom of your garden, where you exchange him bread and water for his priceless masterpieces?"

Hugoson laughed.

"No?" mused the Saint. "Then maybe you have him chained in your attic, where you pass him off as your demented nephew and beat him with rods to keep him working. Or maybe he is your demented nephew?"

"I'm afraid you haven't a very high opinion of my professional ethics, Mr Templar," the publisher said with a smile.

"I apologize," the Saint said. "Of course the truth probably is that Amos Klein is the secret nom de plume of the heir of a dukedom whose father would promptly disinherit him if he knew his son had ever sunk so low as to set pen to any paper less dignified than a legal document. You're merely protecting his good name and his inheritance . . . not that he'll need either, considering the fortune he must have been stacking up over the past couple of years."

"Now you're closer to the mark. But I'm afraid the truth's not nearly as picturesque as you've imagined it." Hugoson's face darkened. "As a matter of fact, the truth's not nearly so bright, either. To be honest, I've been wanting to speak with you about the facts ever since I found out who you are."

"Well, when do I find out the facts—on my twenty-first birthday?"

Hugoson leaned closer, though the precaution seemed scarcely necessary in the combined din of the cinema's mob and the normal uproar of Piccadilly Circus.

"I'll have to speak with you alone. Maybe you'd be so kind as to . . ."

While Hugoson was in mid-sentence, a trio of young men, all fashionably dressed and looking more or less alike, descended on him and proceeded to hustle him away towards a small canebrake of microphones. The essence of the young men's babble was that he was to be favoured immediately with an interview. Hugoson, looking both appalled and flattered at such apparently unwonted attention, called to Simon over his shoulder, "Don't go away, please! It's urgent that I talk to you."

Simon himself was accosted by a gaggle of reporters and photographers who recognized him, but by stubbornly insisting that he had nothing relevant to say, he disposed of them quickly and sauntered towards the tape recorders whose reels were turning in readiness to preserve Mr Finlay Hugoson's words for posterity. But on the way to Mr Hugoson's vicinity he was distracted by the discovery that the stars of the evening's film, *Sunburst Five*, were being questioned in front of cameras almost directly on the street. Rip Savage, as the craggily handsome portrayer of Charles Lake had purportedly been christened by a mother of great foresight and astonishing perception of infant character, was grinning determinedly alongside Carol Henley, whose matching smile looked as if it could not have been blasted off with twice the black powder expended in her last four very explosive films.

"Mr Savage," a Tuxedoed interviewer was asking, "what do you like best about playing Charles Lake?"

"The money."

The interviewer was taken aback by Savage's brash honesty, which had been observed to increase after his payment for each successive film, and turned his attention to Carol Henley.

"Carol, it's said that you're being stereotyped in the Lake pictures. What comment do you have on that?"

Carol's smile never faltered as she hesitated in order to puzzle over the question's meaning.

"Well, goodness," she finally wriggled with breathless rapture, "thank you very much!"

Simon smiled and went to see how his new acquaintance was doing. He gleaned from the rather bellicose tones of the interviewing reporters, even before he could hear their questions, that they were finding the publisher uncooperative.

"Well, Mr Hugoson," he found one saying, "will you at least tell us whether or not Mr Klein has another Lake book on the drawing board."

"On the writing table, more probably," Hugoson replied, in what apparently was an effort to lighten the mood of the inquisition.

The effort failed, as the pettish tone of another reporter attested.

"Are we to take that as an answer, Mr Hugoson, or just as a quip?"

Hugoson's thinning smile withdrew beneath his rectangular moustache.

"Mr Klein is working on a new Lake book," he said precisely.

"Will it be made into a film?"

Hugoson's smile poked its nose tentatively out of the brush.

"I fervently hope so."

A new reporter leaned forward to make himself heard.

"How is it Amos Klein never attends these premieres?"

"I can't comment on that."

"But he does live in England, doesn't he?"

"I can't comment on Mr Klein's private life. I'm very sorry."

There was a brief crescendo of protest from the men of the press, to whom the publisher's reticence on the subject of his prize author was nothing new.

"Surely there's no harm in telling us something about him, Mr Hugoson!"

"You must have met Klein personally," another said. "What's he like?"

"Is he married?"

"Could you just give us some idea of his age?"

"And why all this mystery about him . . ."

Hugoson, looking badgered as well as badgerish, shook his head stubbornly.

"No comment."

"Is the secrecy just a gimmick to arouse public interest?"

"No comment."

As the reporters shouted more questions, all of which received the publisher's "no comment," the Saint noticed that Carol Henley was darting a helpless look at him over her beautiful bare shoulder as she was whisked away by a whole tribe of retainers towards a waiting limousine. She said something to Starnmeck, the producer, who gestured over the heads of the crowd for Simon to join them. It was at that point that Saintly dedication to the discovery and exploration of mysterious byways had to stand and do battle with the more purely human desire to see more of Carol Henley's bare shoulders. But bare female shoulders of acceptable age are not terribly different one from another, particularly when one has enjoyed as many varied views of them as Simon Templar had; anyhow, Carol Henley's were not likely to change radically in the next hour or two, whereas Finlay Hugoson's apparently desperate need to communicate might.

Even so, Simon felt with some regret that he had very possibly chosen the drabber of the two alternatives as he waved good-bye to Carol and Starnmeck and saw the great gleaming black bubble of their car top lose itself in a swirl of other metallic bubbles. He had no logical reason to believe that his contact with Hugoson would expose him to anything more intriguing than some unoriginal recital of a businessman's woes. But the Saint would never have survived and prospered so spectacularly if he had not possessed some of the qualities of gambler and clairvoyant, and tonight he was willing to chance the exceptional physique of Carol Henley against the possibility of what his sixth sense told him might come from Mr Finlay Hugoson.

"Let's take a cab to my flat and have something to drink," Hugoson said.

He was breathless and bedraggled after his encounter with the now completely alienated reporters, a little like a dazed boxer stumbling out of the centre of the ring into the arms of his trainer.

"I appreciate the invitation," Simon answered, "but there's the party at the Savoy. It'd be rather rude for me to pass it up, don't you think? You're a part of this whole shindig, but I'm an invited guest."

The publisher shook his head as he led the Saint towards the curb.

"Those post-premiere affairs are ghastly. Great masses of people showing off for one another like a lot of painted Hottentots. Frightfully depressing!"

"I know," Simon said, "but at least I ought to put in an appearance. Starnmeck was good enough to invite me to the film; I suppose I should pay the price."

Hugoson scratched his moustache nervously.

"As you wish. But I hope you'll be satisfied with a brief appearance and have energy left for a talk with me. There's . . . there's a chance of considerable profit in it for you."

The Saint looked at his small, badger-like acquaintance with new interest.

"If there's one thing I never lack, it's energy," he said, "and if there's one commodity I never have enough of, it's profit—as long, of course, as it's dishonestly earned. I hope you don't have any illusions about my taking up a literary career."

"Not at all. I think I understand your interest."

"Good. We can run over to the Savoy in my car, and then have our talk."

He handed the doorman a ticket.

"Right away, Mr Templar."

The Saint's car was brought promptly, and he took advantage of the short drive to the hotel to sound the publisher out.

"I assume your pal Amos Klein is uppermost in your mind at the moment," he said.

Hugoson darted him a quick glance before answering, but apparently decided that even the Saint, whose private sources of information were popularly reputed to rival those of most national security agencies, could not know the facts of this matter.

"Of course," he said, and then he paused.

"What's all this 'no comment'?" Simon asked.

Even while speeding through the post-theatre traffic of Trafalgar Square, he was as relaxed as most men would have been drowsing at home with the evening paper. Finlay Hugoson clutched the armrest and watched Simon's impossibly near misses of other vehicles with strained admiration.

"I was merely being evasive with the reporters," the publisher said.

"That was fairly obvious. The question is, why? If you want to tell me, that is."

Hugoson's mind seemed to be promptly taken off the rampaging armada of taxis by dour thoughts of his professional problems. He sat back and folded his arms.

"Can you guess what I made out of publishing *The History of the 38th Regiment Hertfordshire Veteran Volunteer Infantry*, morocco bound, with sixty glorious colour plates?"

Simon grinned.

"Obviously not one single family in the UK could afford to be without a copy," he said with an appearance of mental calculation. "I should think you must have cleared at least, say, sixty thousand pounds."

Finlay Hugoson showed no overt signs of amusement at the Saint's whimsy.

"I took a net loss of almost four thousand," he said. "And how much would you guess I was enriched by *Birds of Western Australia*, with thirty-five full-page photographic plates, each copy numbered and signed by the author—who incidentally was my wife's brother?"

"Was it out in time for the Christmas gift trade?" Simon asked.

Hugoson grimly wrung his hands.

"Printers' strike. We missed Christmas by two weeks."

"Doesn't sound good," said the Saint.

"Net loss of two thousand. At least the libraries wanted that one."

"Well, cheer up," Simon said. "If you'd got it out in time for Christmas you might have broken even."

"Wonderful," groaned Hugoson. "What more could a publisher ask?"

"With your flair for picking winners, I'd say breaking even might call for a real celebration."

"And then," Hugoson said, "along came the first Charles Lake novel."

"And?"

"They're making me rich."

"That's nice."

"They're making me richer than I ever dreamed I'd be."

"That's even nicer."

"But . . ."

"But what?" the Saint asked encouragingly. When the other hesitated, he continued. "And that still doesn't explain all the 'no comments.'"

There was no chance for explanation then, because the Saint's skilful navigation had brought them to the Embankment entrance of the Savoy, where most of the horde of people in any way connected with *Sunburst Five* had already disembarked and made their way to the private rooms set aside for their jubilation. Simon and Hugoson found one or two hundred of them in the early phases of that intoxication which is never quite so swiftly induced or magnificently sustained as by the presence of an unlimited supply of free booze. The raiment of the females, as well as that of some of the males, would have made the finery of the best-dressed birds of western Australia seem pale in comparison, and the gushing and shameless politicking of both sexes would have made the first day of the mating season on Seal Island sound like the slumbrous murmurs of teatime at the old folks' home.

Simon failed to spot Starnmeck or Carol Henley, and nodded wryly towards the impenetrable mob pressed along the bar.

"This visit may be even briefer than I'd planned."

"The briefer the better," Hugoson agreed. "This is one aspect of making a fortune I could very well do without."

The melancholy prognosis was promptly justified, as he was swallowed up in the gilt and purple plumage of a woman of impressive stature who swooped down on him with shrill cries of delight.

"Why, Finlay, you naughty thing! We were sure you'd run out on us, probably off to see that author of yours! Come now! You simply must tell us where you're hiding him!"

Simon, knowing full well that he himself would become the prey of similar predatory onslaughts as soon as he was recognized, pried Hugoson from his female assailant and steered him through a suffocating haze of cigarette smoke and other hot air towards the door.

"Had enough?" he asked.

"I never saw her before in my life," Hugoson gasped.

"Public acclaim is the reward of guessing right," Simon said. "If you're enjoying it, don't let me interrupt the fun."

"Please! Let's get out. Here comes another one."

Hugoson lived in a town house just off Park Lane, in the kind of street notable for its large cars and small well-shampooed dogs. It was almost midnight, and some of the dogs were leading their masters and mistresses on pre-bedtime walks. Those of the large cars which were not garaged shone in the light of street lamps like brightly polished gemstones. The great stone facades of the buildings created a sense of solidity, dignity, and abiding success not so newly achieved as to be embarrassing to the kind of people who only respect success if it is not indecently recent.

"A very suitable location for England's most prosperous publisher," Simon said.

He and Hugoson had left the car and were climbing the steps towards one of the massive brass-trimmed doors.

"Publishing's a gentleman's game, you know," said Hugoson wryly. "I've lived here for years. Only difference is, now I can afford the rent."

He fitted his key into the lock, opened the door, and felt for a switch.

"Thought I left a light on," he said. "Well, no wonder: the switch is on, but the bulb must have burnt out. Have you a match?"

"I don't carry them since I quit smoking," Simon apologized.

"Doesn't matter. I'll just—"

Even the Saint's superb reflexes, which rarely left him at a disadvantage, were of no use to him in the totally unexpected onslaught that followed. In the same instant that he heard Finlay Hugoson's pained grunt, he felt a crushing blow on the back of his own head, and the darkness of the hall merged into a deeper black.

3

The Saint had never been fond of things on grounds of rarity alone. He had never been excited by eclipses of the moon nor had his pulse quickened at the sight of a six-legged calf. But of all the things which the Saint did not like because of their rarity, he liked least the rare experience of being bashed with some firm artifact on the back of his skull.

As he woke up on the floor of Mr Finlay Hugoson's house off Park Lane, his mind naturally turned to the subject of blows on the head (his own head in particular), to the alertness and skill which had made such blows a rarity in his life till then, and to the means by which he would make such blows an even greater rarity in the future.

But such meditations, however fruitful they might be in the long view, had to give way to more immediate considerations. The Saint knew only that he was lying on the floor of some dark silent place. Instinct and experience made him avoid making any sound or movement at first beyond the slow opening of his eyes; before revealing that he was conscious, he wanted to be certain that his attacker was not still present. Having made reasonably sure of that fact, he ventured to sit up. The dull throbbing in his head suddenly became a sharp ache, as if his whole brain had shifted position inside his cranium, but the moan that broke the silence did not come from his throat. It came, presumably, from Finlay Hugoson, somewhere else in the darkness.

"Are you awake?" Simon asked, unable to think of any question or remark which would not sound equally ridiculous in the circumstances.

The only response from Hugoson was an inarticulate groan. The Saint got to his feet, trying to force his pain and his anger at whoever had caused it out of his consciousness.

He recalled that they had just entered the house, and the hall light wouldn't go on. Hugoson had been looking for another switch, and there had to be one, in some room opening off the hall. Simon found a wall, groped along it to a door frame, almost fell over something sprawled across the threshold, and finally found a switch on the inside which turned on the bulbs of a crystal chandelier in the centre of the ceiling of the room beyond.

The room was just as solidly elegant as he had expected it to be, and just as severely disordered. Drawers from an antique writing table were upside down on the floor. Sheets of paper and envelopes were strewn on the rug. The owner of the ransacked property was also still lying in the doorway, and Simon turned quickly back to him when he saw that the side of Hugoson's face was covered with blood. Using his handkerchief, the Saint ascertained that the wound was not serious, but was no more than an abrasion caused by a glancing blow on the side of the head.

"Nice way your retainers have of welcoming you home," Simon said as Hugoson's eyes flickered open.

"What happened?" the publisher groaned.

"I'm hoping you can tell me . . . beyond the obvious fact that we were both swatted on the sconce."

Hugoson's eyes opened wider, as if in suddenly realized fear. He tried to raise his head and fell back.

"I feel as if my skull's fractured," he gasped.

"It very well could be. You may have a concussion, so lie still. There's no chance of catching our playmates right now anyway. I never even got a look at them. Did you?"

"No," answered Hugoson weakly. "I just know that something hit me. What . . . what have they done?"

"Just a little housekeeping," said the Saint. "When you get well enough to sit up, you'll be amazed at what a few thoughtful changes have done for your decor."

Hugoson tried again to move, but shut his eyes and winced.

"I'd better get you a doctor," the Saint told him. "Any preference?"

"Later," Hugoson mumbled. "First . . . I've got to know . . . what they took."

"I'd be glad to tell you," Simon replied, "but it's a little difficult since I don't have any idea what was here before they came to call. Where'd you keep the family treasures? I'll check there first."

"No," said Hugoson. "I don't keep any money or valuables in the house, except some rare books in glass cases in the library, just off to the right."

Simon moved to take a look at the room which Hugoson indicated with a feeble motion of his hand.

"But there's not much point even checking that," the publisher continued. "I'm afraid . . . those weren't the sort of things they were after."

The remark brought the Saint up short, but not before he had seen that the books in their cases were undisturbed.

"You're right," he said. "You mean—these guests were expected?"

"In a way. Yes. Please, check my desk—in the library. Did they get into that?"

25

"They did," Simon reported, after a moment. "It looks as if they took it apart with a crowbar."

"They were probably looking everywhere for the key," Hugoson called, "but I took the precaution of carrying it with me."

"I'm afraid the power of locks and keys is greatly over-estimated," the Saint called back.

He was fingering the splintered wood of several drawers in the library desk. Papers had been tossed aside at random until a certain file folder had been uncovered. The folder was open on the desk. Whatever it had once held was gone. On the tab of the folder were printed the words "Amos Klein."

"That's what they were after," quavered Hugoson's voice.

The Saint looked up and saw that the publisher had made his way to the library door, and was standing there, clinging feebly to the jamb.

"This?" Simon asked, holding up the folder.

"Yes. Personal correspondence with . . . with Amos Klein."

"Just over-eager autograph collectors, or what?"

"They wanted his address primarily. I'm sure of it."

"There must be easier ways of getting it than this," hazarded the Saint.

"There aren't. Only I know it."

Hugoson's voice trailed off, so Simon helped him into a chair.

"Your employees must have learned his address," Simon said then. "Your secretary? And why all the secrecy anyway?"

"One thing at a time," Hugoson said tiredly. "In the first place, I correspond from my office with Klein only to post office boxes, using fake names. Nobody could find him through information in my office files. The people who are looking for him already discovered that; they broke into my publishing house offices a couple of days ago. That, in fact, was my main reason for wanting to talk to you. I realized somebody was out to find Klein by any means necessary."

The Saint, lounging against the wall, held up one hand and interrupted.

"Just one question, to put at least some perspective in this picture: why should Amos Klein be so difficult to find in the first place?"

"Because I don't want him to be found," Hugoson said.

"Why?"

"Because . . . because of several things, but primarily because I want to protect my investment."

"He doesn't sound like an investment—he sounds like a pure asset."

"Whatever you want to call it . . ."

"The goose that lays the golden eggs?" Simon suggested. "You've hidden it away so nobody can steal it?"

"Right," said Hugoson. "Exactly." He noted Simon's almost unbelieving and somehow accusing stare. "Well, you can't blame me! I'm a capitalist. I was dangerously close to being bankrupt when Klein came along, and I've no intention of letting anybody take him away from me. I don't want to publish literature any more. I just want to be a millionaire!"

"A laudable ambition," the Saint said. "But you have a rather extreme way of protecting yourself. I'm beginning to think you may really have your boy Klein locked up in a hen coop somewhere. What does he think about this?"

"The arrangement suits him fine. He has no desire for publicity. I couldn't keep him away from the world if he wanted to be known, obviously."

The Saint surveyed the wreckage of the desk and shook his head

"I don't know," he mused. "If this is the way publishers are competing with one another these days, I wouldn't be the least bit surprised to hear they were holding writers prisoner."

"If they are publishers," Hugoson said mysteriously.

Simon gave him a hard look.

"You mean the competition? The ones who're so anxious to find Klein?"

"Yes."

"Well, if it's not a publisher, who is it?"

"I can't think," muttered Hugoson.

"Now listen," the Saint said a little irritably, "apparently you had some notion of getting me to help you, so what's the point of playing ring around the rosy?"

"I was going to try to hire you to protect Klein . . . and his identity."

"You'd have failed," Simon replied. "I don't hire myself out. As a matter of fact, if I didn't have a personal interest in this situation, in the form of an aching skull, I'd walk out in indignation."

Hugoson brightened. "You mean you will help?"

"I've no intention of letting anybody cosh me and get away with it. If in the process of my personal vendetta I incidentally happen to help keep your coffers full, that's all right with me. So tell me everything you know, and I'll call your doctor and be on my way."

"On your way where?"

"To get to Amos Klein before your competitors get there."

4

It was a pleasant surprise to learn that Amos Klein worked and did a good deal of his living in a cottage at Burnham, only about forty-five minutes' drive from the centre of London. Simon had envisioned himself pursuing adventure and vengeance into the jungles of Borneo or up the peaks of the Andes. The chimerical Mr Klein's residence in England was a convenience which the Saint not only appreciated but took immediate advantage of. With only as much delay as it took to accept Hugoson's offer of a restorative drink, he got back in his car and was soon driving along the M4 motorway in the direction of Slough.

But while he was grateful for Klein's proximity, he could not see much more in the affair to his advantage. Aside from the astonishing revelation of the length to which modern publishing competition seemed prepared to go, with burglary and mayhem a merely routine step towards finding and propositioning a popular but elusive author, it did not promise any of the exhilarating twists of a typical Saintly crusade against some particularly vile species of injustice. Of course, there had now been created an obligation to find the perpetrator of the clout he had received and repay the blow with interest, but that was hardly an electrifying inspiration.

As Simon had said to Hugoson as they parted, "To think that I gave up Carol Henley's company for some slope-shouldered little twerp with ink on his nose."

Hugoson, who had seemed about to say something else, smiled wanly through the drawn grimace of his headache.

"You'll live to eat that description, anyway," the publisher said. "And who knows? You might even fall for him."

"One of those, eh?" said the Saint. "Well, thanks for the warning."

"Ring me up! I wish I felt up to going with you. And give . . . Amos my regards."

Disappointingly, when the Saint had left the M4 and found his way through dark country roads to the proper cottage, according to Hugoson's directions, it seemed as if he might not be able to give Amos Klein regards or anything else that night. The cottage, set alone in a densely wooded patch at the end of a lane, was completely dark.

Simon's first thought was that the group who had been showing such an extraordinary interest in making the acquaintance of Finlay Hugoson's gold-ovulating goose might have beaten him to the place and already roared away with the author in a cloud of advance royalty offers. On the other hand, it was just as possible that Klein had gone to bed quite peacefully. Simon's apprehension about the eventuality of a kidnapping was eased when he quietly tested the front door and found it locked. He rapped and waited. Then he heard an irregular bumping sound coming faintly from the rear of the place. It was not any sort of sound that one would expect to be made by a man alone in the middle of the night, and it did not last long.

Instantly, the Saint was balanced like an alerted leopard, ready for anything. He moved with the silent stealth of a cat around the sides of the cottage, until he had satisfied himself that there was no one else in the garden. Then the bumping sounds, which clearly came from within the house, began again. Simon started to knock on the back door, near which he was now poised, but something caught his eye which he had not seen before: a razor edge of light at French windows to his left. The apparent darkness of the cottage, then, was due at least in part to thick hangings inside the windows. Simon moved quickly to take a look through the curtains just in time to see what appeared to be the demise of the object of his trip.

A dark-suited man, seated in front of a typewriter, was slipping slowly forward and to the floor, a long knife projecting from between his shoulder blades.

The Saint's automatic was already in his hand. Almost simultaneously with blasting away the lock on the French windows with a single shot, he kicked the windows open and, without making a target of himself, prepared to incapacitate anything hostile. But all he saw was a most unhostile and terrified-looking girl leaning back against the opposite wall. She was standing, her ankles lashed together, her wrists apparently in the same condition behind her. A white towel was tied around her head, restricting her powers of communication to a series of mouselike squeaks.

The room had only one exit into the rest of the cottage, and Simon dashed to that open door. A glance down the central hall told him that the front entrance was closed and bolted from inside. He had heard no sound of the nearby kitchen door being opened, which could only mean that the wielder of the knife was in all probability still in the house. He did not, however, have time to plan at his own pace what he would do about the situation because suddenly a bullet slammed into the lintel above his head, accompanied by the loud report of a pistol which would have sent a man with nerves of anything less than pure platinum jumping at least five feet.

Simon whirled, ducking, and saw the captive girl, her back to him, holding a revolver upside down in her roped hands. She was hopping towards the open French windows, the nose of her weapon waving like the nozzle of a garden hose as she fired it again—this time into a picture on the wall at a quite comfortable distance from the Saint.

"Hold it!" he shouted at her. "I'm a friend."

Her third shot, remarkably near his feet considering that both he and she were moving and that she was not even looking in his direction, said more about her scepticism than any number of words.

"Cut that out so I can catch the people who did this," he yelled at her.

In his lunge to catch her arm, while at the same time he tried to keep his eye on the hall door for a possible flanking attack, he almost fell over the body of the man who had been seated at the typewriter. Simon's foot, instead of meeting the solid resistance of bone and flesh, sent the man's form skidding across the floor as if it had been a mere bag of straw.

And that was more or less what it was. It was no man. It was a well-dressed dummy.

The Saint had no time to inspect the oddity for the moment. His attention was drawn irresistibly to the pistol which could at any moment, if only by sheer accident, put a hole in his head. One of his hands closed on the girl's arm while the other, after shoving his own gun into the band of his trousers, snatched the weapon out of her hands.

"I think we can put things on a more friendly basis without that," he said.

The girl could still only squeak. Simon, keeping a wary eye on the doorway, loosened the gag and tore it from her mouth with no great attempt at gentleness. Now that she was free to speak, she suddenly seemed to have lost her desire even to make incoherent noises. She merely stared at him, breathing hard, with a mixture of uncertain fear and defiance that he found most attractive. She would have been attractive even without the display of courage—her face beautiful and proud, her jade eyes looking out at the world from under a cap of short black hair.

"Now," said the Saint, "how many of us are there, not counting Pinocchio on the floor?"

"Who are you?" the girl demanded.

"I asked the first question, and I'll add another: who are you? I'd like an answer to both—fast!"

He encouraged her with a waggle of the gun he had taken over.

"There's nobody else here," she said, shrinking back. Then she added quickly, "But I've called the police. They'll be here any minute."

Simon, who had been critically studying the girl's bonds from various angles, relaxed against the wall.

"I'm afraid that doesn't frighten me," he said. "In the first place, I'm crazy about the police. In the second place, I happen to know this cottage doesn't have a phone."

The girl frowned.

"How do you know anything like that?"

"Hugoson told me."

The girl looked momentarily relieved, and then she tensed again.

"Have you hurt him?"

"Hugoson? Of course not. We're practically blood brothers. Or bruise brothers, anyway. Incidentally, I know you've worked your hands out of those ropes, so you might as well put them in front of you where I can admire them."

She stared at him for an instant with surprise, before she screwed her face up petulantly and let the ropes slip to the floor.

"You're very observant," she said.

Simon nodded agreement.

"And you're quite an escape artist," he told her. "Except I'm not sure you should get full credit for escaping from ropes you put on yourself."

This time she showed real amazement.

"How'd you know that?"

The Saint smiled.

"I'm very observant. Unfortunately, though, I'm not always observant enough, otherwise I'd never have burst in here to rescue a dummy and a girl who for some obscure reason likes to spend her evenings tying herself up with sash cord."

The girl was rubbing her wrists.

"The knot got stuck," she said, "luckily for you. If the loop had come loose I'd have had my gun right side up and potted you between the eyes." She nodded towards her revolver, which he still held almost absentmindedly in his hand. "Are you going to shoot me?"

"Not in any vital organs, anyway." He put the pistol in his jacket and folded his arms, noting the heap of lipstick-marked cigarette stubs in the ashtray beside the typewriter. "Now, Annie Oakley, what are your other talents besides fancy marksmanship and rope tricks?"

The girl looked at the typewriter, and then at Simon.

"Didn't Hugoson tell you?"

"Tell me what?" the Saint asked unguardedly.

The girl hesitated, and then, with an exasperated explosion of breath, put her hands on her lips.

"That I'm Amos Klein."

CHAPTER TWO:

HOW AMOS KLEIN WAS
PROPOSITIONED AND GALAXY
ROSE WAS BRUSHED OFF

1

"That's a pretty name for a girl," said the Saint with extraordinary restraint.

Amos Klein pushed strands of raven hair from her flushed forehead.

"My mother had a poetic soul. And now, if you're dying to introduce yourself, don't let me stop you."

"Gladly. I'm Simon Templar."

The girl's face showed surprised recognition of the name, and she looked at him more closely.

"The Saint?" she asked.

He nodded.

"There was poetry in my background, too."

"Or a pretty far-fetched imagination." She indicated the shattered French windows. "For a Saint, you have a pretty violent way of coming to call."

Simon closed the windows and drew the curtain back across them.

"I'll treat you to a repair job," he said.

"Would you mind? I'm tired of hopping about like a human pogo stick, and as long as I have a man around I might as well make use of him."

She was talking about the rope which still bound her ankles together. Simon knelt down to release her.

"A very wise attitude," he agreed. "As a matter of fact, I was encouraged to come here to be useful. Finlay Hugoson and I were together at the premiere of your latest epic, and when we dropped by his flat we ran into a couple of uninvited guests who hadn't expected him to come home till after the party. They were looking for your address, and they got away with it. Hugoson thought it would be a good idea if I got right down here to protect you . . . or keep you from signing up with some competitor of his."

"Why didn't he come?" she asked.

"He would have, but he was indisposed after being conked on the head by your fans."

"Fans?"

"The ones who're so anxious to find you." Simon had finished untying the ropes, and he stood up. "You tie a good knot," he said.

"Summer sailor." She looked apologetically down at the tight-fitting faded jeans and the sloppy sweat shirt she was wearing. "Excuse me if I'm dressed like one, but I wasn't expecting company, friendly or otherwise."

"I'd planned to announce myself in a more conventional way," the Saint told her, "but your little charade completely took me in."

He went over to look at the dummy with the knife in its back.

"That's Warlock," Amos Klein explained as she began to straighten up the room.

"Warlock?" Simon repeated. "He's the top villain in your books, right?"

"Right. He and his cohorts were keeping me prisoner in a cellar. And Dunlap Brodie . . . he's the nice boy whose mother was killed by SWORD . . . slips me this knife. So I'm going to kill Warlock when he comes to torture me. He's sitting down at the console to turn up the hypnotic knob when I let him have it in the back . . . from ten paces, with my hands tied. And just then you come along and let me have it, right in the back door."

"Well," said Simon, "at least you can write the damage off to research."

"You're right. I like to try things out to see if they're just barely possible. Every little experience adds realism."

She was picking the dummy up off the floor and sitting him in an armchair. Suddenly she stopped, listening.

"Did you hear something?" she whispered.

"No. What?"

She was still frozen in her leaning position over the dummy.

"In the hall."

Simon had not heard anything in the hall, and he did not believe his hostess had heard anything either, but he decided to play along and let her get out of her system whatever it was she had in mind. The knife in the dummy's back had looked very long and very sharp, but Simon turned anyway, like a matador defying a bull with the mockery of his undefended back, and looked towards the hall door. Only a man of supreme confidence in his own luck and skill could have made the move, the Saint was as sure of himself as if he had been going through a routine judo exercise.

"Now," said the girl, "don't move."

At the same time Simon felt the cold point of the knife touch his neck.

"Is that any way for a damsel in distress to treat her knight errant?" he asked coolly. "I'm tempted just to leave you to the wolves . . . but I won't."

The Saint's last three words were accompanied by a move so sudden and so swift that even an attentive observer would have been hard put to say just how the long knife ended up in his hand and exactly what caused the girl who had been holding it only an instant before to be sitting with the wind knocked out of her on the floor.

"You look so surprised," he said amiably. "Wasn't that according to the script?"

"How am I supposed to know you're the Saint?" the girl demanded.

"How am I supposed to know you're Amos Klein?" he retorted. "At least I'm the right sex."

Almost without so much as a glance to his right at the dummy in its chair, Simon carelessly flicked the knife from his fingertips and sent the sharp-pointed blade flying deep into the painted head directly between the eyes.

"I think," the girl gulped, "that for the moment, anyway, I'll just have to trust you."

Simon took her by one hand and hoisted her to her feet.

"In that case, I'll have another try at trusting you."

"Another try?"

"Well I just showed you my good faith by turning my back on you, and look what it got me. And would you blame me for doubting that anything quite as gorgeous as you could be named Amos Klein?"

She gazed at him with a special kind of melting glow which only flattery can produce in the eyes of the human female.

"I not only may learn to trust you—I may learn to love you."

"All things in their seasons," said the Saint agreeably. "And if it makes you feel any more comfortable, I really don't doubt your identity. I know now why Finlay Hugoson made what seemed like a very naughty suggestion that I might fall for you if I came out here."

"He's not supposed to tell anybody I'm a girl. It's in our contract."

She went over to a cabinet in the corner which yielded two glasses and a bottle of Old Curio. Simon looked at the pages of manuscript which lay beside the typewriter.

"How do you do it?" he asked.

"Do what?"

"Write these tough, tough books."

Amos Klein shrugged as she poured the whiskey.

"Something went wrong at the factory, I guess."

"Factory?" the Saint asked.

"The people factory. They ran out of proper girlie ribbons."

"Not from where I'm looking."

She smiled with another glow of pure joy as she handed him his drink.

"You're very sweet. Cheers . . . to trust."

"To trust, Amos." His mouth reacted to the pronunciation of the name as it would have reacted to a large bite of lemon peel. "I just can't call you that, darling."

"All right, call me darling."

They both smiled and drank again.

"Now," the girl said, "could you explain a little more about what's going on—what brought you here? I mean, who's behind all this?"

"First, I'd be much happier if you'd satisfy my curiosity," Simon said. "What's one of the most successful authors in the world doing hiding her light and gender under a bushel out here in the midst of the beech woods?"

"It was partly Finlay's idea. He thought it would help sales—the mystery, you know. And he also thought that the public might not take my books so well if they knew they were written by a woman."

"Maybe, but I doubt there would have been any problem. It didn't hurt Agatha Christie. Hugoson seems very conservative, though."

"He is, and I had personal reasons, too. My family's even more conservative than Finlay, and if they dreamed I was ruining myself for marriage and a life among decent people by writing sex and sadism thrillers they'd cut me off without a penny."

"Then Amos Klein isn't your real name," Simon deduced, with some relief.

"No . . . But when I began publishing these things I was completely dependent on them, and I may be adventurous in imagination but I wasn't particularly willing to face starvation in person."

"But I should think you'd have made a fortune by now, with royalties and movie rights and all that."

"Amos Klein" beamed.

"I have. But there's no point in giving my father an excuse to cancel out an eighty-thousand-pound trust fund just a year before it's released to me. So long as I'm going to be rich, I might as well be filthy rich."

Simon laughed.

"I appreciate that laudable ambition. Where do Mama and Papa think you are now? In finishing school?"

"You are a flatterer," the girl said, tossing her hair. "I'm twenty-four years old, and schools almost finished me a long time ago. My mother's dead, and my father's too preoccupied with his own business to think very deeply about my location as long as I'm not in his way. I keep him satisfied with various stories. I get friends to mail him my letters from highly respectable places. Of course the friends don't know what I'm really doing either. I spent the last three months with a girl friend in Italy who forwarded my mail and thought I was in Spain with a bullfighter."

"And all the time you were here," Simon said.

She drained her glass.

"Working like a galley slave. The nearest thing I've seen to a bullfighter is the postman dodging dogs on his bicycle."

"Which probably explains the frustrated look in your eyes, darling," he remarked.

Darling met his mischievous grin with a determined frown.

"Sir, if you're going to take advantage of a lady's loneliness, I shall have to ask you to leave and never break down my door again."

"You could look at it another way," the Saint suggested. "Maybe I'm the hero who's going to rescue the damsel from the dark castle."

"Maybe so."

Her face had softened, but it immediately became more businesslike.

"Now," she continued, "this is all lots of fun, but shouldn't we get down to work?"

"Fine," Simon agreed. "First, are your other doors and windows locked?"

"Yes. But what a creepy thing to ask! Do you think somebody might try to kidnap me?"

"Maybe you can tell me that. Frankly, the amount I know about this situation is so limited that my guesses would be just that—guesses. If there had been only one man in Hugoson's apartment we'd at least have the possibility of some crackpot autograph hound carrying his hobby to completely nutty extremes. But there were at least two people, so that's out. The other guesses involve newspapermen or unethical publishers, if you can believe that."

The Saint rested himself sidesaddle on the desk. The girl had shoved the dummy out of the armchair onto the floor and flopped down into the cushions herself.

"You're right," she said. "That's pretty far out."

"Any guess seems far out. Unless maybe this whole situation had nothing to do with you as an author at all. But if that were the case, why would the evil ones be tracking you down under the name of Amos Klein? If they were after ransom from your father, for instance, they'd have tried to trace you under your real name, whatever that is."

The girl wrinkled her nose.

"You're not going to tell me the real name?" Simon asked. "I give my word not to let the world in on the secret. 'Darling' is fine, but it could be slightly awkward if I had to introduce you."

"It's Amity," she said, looking wretched. "Amity Little."

"Aha. I see where you got Amos Klein." Simon tried the sound of it, maintaining a strictly straight face. "Amity Little. Sounds like a missionary."

"My father's notion," Amity said. "He's a Quaker. You can see why I'm not terribly keen on telling people—nor on seeing it emblazoned on the jackets of thrillers."

"I do see, darling," said Simon. "Now, to get back to our theories before your mysterious admirers show up here, is it possible they could have started out with a plan to kidnap Amity Little for ransom from her loving father, and then accidentally discovered that Amity Little and Amos Klein were the same? That would seem to promise them even more profit—they could ask Hugoson for ransom as well. And of course one of the last stages in the game would be finding out just where to find Amos Klein."

Amity shook her head. Her eyes narrowed.

"I don't think so," she said very thoughtfully. "I think the real answer might be much weirder than that."

"Well?"

Amity bit her thumbnail, completely absorbed in her musing.

"I wonder . . ." she said.

The Saint shifted his weight impatiently.

"So do I. Button, button, who's got the button?"

"Just a minute," Amity said.

She broke off her introspection and suddenly got to her feet. Going to the desk, she threw open one of the drawers and began burrowing through a deep and disordered pile of papers.

"Bury a bone?" Simon said.

"A letter. There."

Triumphantly, she drew a sheet of paper out of the chaos. Attached to the paper was a cheque. She handed it to Simon, who glanced at the amount of the cheque before reading the letter.

"Fifty thousand pounds," he said in the appreciative tone of a connoisseur of currency in all its forms.

"Before you get excited, read the letter," Amity Little told him.

"Dear Mr Klein . . . enclosed is a cheque for fifty thousand pounds, being half-payment for your writing services, which we are most anxious to acquire. Period of employment, two months. Balance of payment on completion. The work will be secret, most challenging, and is guaranteed to be to your taste. Your cashing this cheque will be regarded as full acceptance of the contract as stated above, whereupon you will be contacted and given further instructions." The Saint's reaction at the large black flourished signature showed only a moment's beat before he read it aloud. "Warlock."

He looked inquiringly and unbelievingly at Amity Little, who nodded confirmation.

"Warlock," she repeated. "The arch villain in my Charles Lake books. And look underneath the name." She looked over Simon's shoulder and moved the tip of a slim finger along the word as she spelled out the block capitals in which it was printed. "SWORD"

"Your fictional organization for world evil."

"Secret World Organization for Retribution and Destruction. And Warlock's the boss."

"You actually got this in the mail?" Simon asked.

"Yes. Forwarded by Finlay. He sends mail on addressed to Amos Klein unopened."

Simon looked at the date of the letter.

"You got it a month ago?"

"Approximately."

"What have you done about it?"

"Nothing."

"How could you resist?"

"Cashing the cheque, you mean?"

"Not necessarily," Simon said. "But at least trying to find out something about where it came from."

"Well, for one thing it gave me the creeps," Amity Little replied.

"Understandably. It must be a bit like seeing yourself walk in the door."

"Yes. And I'm pretty tied down by the fact that I can't let anybody know who I am. Of course I don't have a bank account in the name of Amos Klein."

"Didn't you even call the bank this is drawn on?"

"Why?"

The Saint studied the cheque more closely as he answered.

"To see if anyone really has an account in the name of Warlock."

Amity tossed the idea off with a sweeping gesture.

"Don't be ridiculous! There isn't any Warlock, except in my head. Obviously whoever sent this is some sort of nut!"

The Saint held up his hand for silence, and turned his head to listen.

"Who may be coming up your drive right now," he said softly.

2

"I don't hear anything," Amity Little said.

"I have rather exceptional hearing," the Saint said. "Let's have a look out of the front windows."

She led him through the house to one of the heavily draped windows in the dining room.

"You mean that car?" she whispered, listening. "I hear them turning around in my drive all the time. I'm at the end of the lane, so it's the natural place."

Simon had edged a curtain aside enough to peer out.

"Do they often have blue lights flashing?" he inquired.

"Oh!"

Amity looked as a man in uniform stepped from the car and came up the walk. A moment later he knocked at the front door.

"Somebody must have reported the shots," Simon said.

A fat-faced stocky constable stood on the steps when Amity opened the door.

"Good evening, ma'am, sir," he said pleasantly. "P. C. Jarvis, Burnham police."

"Yes?"

"We've something peculiar come up," said the man. "The Inspector asked me to request that you please come down to the station."

"What for, at an hour like this?" Simon asked. "Does he want someone to sing him to sleep?"

"There's reason to believe that some kind of attack might be made on this house."

"What reason?"

"I couldn't say, sir. I'm only following orders. It seems there's some funny things going on, and I wouldn't want to alarm you, but the Inspector says it's for your own protection."

Simon and Amity exchanged glances, and the Saint's eyes darted back to a ring he had noticed on the officer's left hand. It was a large golden ring ornately carved in Florentine style.

"That's very kind of the Inspector," he said to the policeman. "If we're in danger, maybe you'd better come inside so we can shut the door."

Constable Jarvis held back, protesting that he was not sure of any such great or immediate danger, but the Saint, with fingers very much like steel clamps not yet exerting a tenth of their potential pressure, took the man's arm and urged him into the hall with firm friendliness. Amity closed the door and bolted it.

"Can we offer you a drink?" she asked.

"Not on duty, ma'am. Thanks just the same." The policeman looked rather longingly over his shoulder at the locked door. "It'd be best if you could just come along now, so the Inspector can explain everything to you himself."

"Is Charlie Huggins with you?" Simon asked.

"No, sir."

"Too bad. I'd like to see old Charlie. Will he be at the station if we come down?"

"Huggins?" the policeman asked.

The Saint became openly suspicious.

"Constable Huggins," he said.

Constable Jarvis broke into a broad grin.

"Oh, Huggins! Of course. He's not on duty this evening, but I'll give him your regards tomorrow."

"That's very good of you. Please do it . . . as soon as you wake up."

On the words "wake up" the Saint's fist blurred into the tender flab of the other's jaw like an upswung sledgehammer. Without even a groan the man dropped to the floor.

Amity was aghast.

"What are you doing?" she squeaked.

"The ring's suspicious enough on a country constable, but I know for a fact there's no such person as Charlie Huggins here, because Charlie Huggins is a bartender friend of mine in Chelsea."

"So who's this?" Amity asked, pointing at the limp plump form on the floor.

"Warlock?" Simon asked.

"Oh, that's really too much!"

"I agree. And there may have been somebody with him in that car, so let's take the other way out and see what we can see. Our friend here will be happy to rest till we get back."

They went back to the writing room, turned off the lights, and Simon parted the curtains to peek out of the French windows. A very tall, very brawny figure in a uniform and cap similar to the one worn by P. C. Jarvis appeared in the light of the quarter moon.

"It's a little crowded out here," he murmured. "Let's take the front way after all."

"What was it?" Amity asked as he towed her through the hall.

"He looked a bit like one of Dr Frankenstein's play toys. I'm afraid we may as well admit to ourselves that your ivory tower is under attack, and that we're at least temporarily on the defensive. Here's your gun back, but let's not start killing people unless it's absolutely necessary."

Amity Little gave a low moan. "Killing people?"

Simon's hand was on the front door lock preparatory to opening it.

"It shouldn't bother you," he said. "You killed at least thirty in your last book, and you came pretty close to bumping me off tonight, so let's not get emotional. Show you're a real man, Amos! Let's make a dash for my car."

He took the girl's hand in his and ran silently across the grass. The police car, which appeared to be empty, was only partly blocking the driveway. His first concern was to get Amity to safety, to protect her from capture; with that accomplished, he could go to work on the group which was taking such an extraordinary interest in her literary career. The drastic measures to find her, the elaborate impersonation of police complete with official car, not to mention the offer of fifty thousand pounds, all postulated an organization and capital resources beyond the capacity of mere cranks. And that being the case, it was doubtful that shooting it out with a pair of bogus cops on the spot would be likely to settle anything, although it might rid the world of two of its less attractive inhabitants.

"Get in," Simon whispered.

Amity obeyed as he opened the driver's side of his car. She scrambled past the steering wheel to make room for him. As he turned the key in the ignition, the front door of Amity's cottage opened and the bulk of the second imitation policeman was outlined against the dim light inside, having evidently discovered the broken French windows and taken advantage of them to enter and come through. Simon slammed the gear lever into reverse and stepped on the gas to send the car screeching into the road.

But then a curious thing happened. Even as the engine took hold and the car started back, he lost all interest in driving. He felt a sort of cool and queer-smelling breeze in his face, and had just enough ability for analytical thought left in his consciousness to tell him that some somnific gas must be coming through the heater vents.

"Simon . . ."

It was Amity mumbling his name groggily as she slumped down into her seat, her head flopping over against his arm. But the arm was as heavy as iron, and more debilitating even than that was the nonchalance with which his spirit insisted on treating the whole event, no matter how desperately a small and helpless part of his mind told him he ought to resist.

He could no more avoid losing consciousness than a stone could have floated on the sea whose surf hissed in his ears. As greater and greater depths of unawareness came between him and the surface world of light and sound, he caught a last rippling glimpse of forms—the faces of men looking down at him, like white grinning masks bobbing above the dark cloth of uniforms, cloth like night sky, where constellations of silver buttons bloomed like stars.

3

Simon Templar thought he had been dreaming about a play taking place in a setting as vast as a football stadium; on the stage more and more people entered, some actors and some not actors, until reality was so confused with make-believe that the whole scene was in milling chaos . . .

And then, as brighter light sifted into his eyes, the Saint saw the stage become smaller, like the plush little private theatre of some eighteenth-century nobleman, and its intimate red velvet curtains had parted, and there was a beautiful young woman waiting to greet the audience.

"Good morning, Mr Klein."

Simon focussed his eyes and realized that he was in a bed of proportions almost as extravagant as those of the stage in his dream. It was a canopied four-poster bed with curtains all around. The curtains at its foot were being held apart by the gorgeous creature who had spoken. She could not have been much over twenty, her face was classic perfection, and her long hair was like faintly tarnished silver.

"Good morning, blessed damosel," Simon murmured.

His poetic greeting was not entirely due to romanticism or his admittedly muddled head. His mind, clicking rapidly back into action like a computer centre after a power failure, was recollecting the circumstances that had brought him here. He wanted to stall the girl while he woke up more thoroughly and took stock of the situation.

"I hope that's nice," she said.

"What?"

"What you said: blasted . . ."

"Blessed?" Simon offered.

"Blessed dam . . . what?"

"Blessed damosel. It's a kind of angel, you might say. I never was completely clear on it myself. 'She looked out from the gold bar of heaven,' it says in the poem. They must have some pretty fancy pubs there."

The girl allowed herself to smile as she opened the curtains on either side of the bed, flooding it with morning sunlight.

"That does sound nice," she said.

She wore a sleeveless white top and skin-tight stretch pants of a kind of pink iridescent silken material. Her figure was positively baroque in its voluptuousness, and her swinging movements around the bed did a great deal towards lifting the Saint's metabolism back to normal.

"I suppose it would be too much to guess I've gone to heaven?" he said. "Not that I haven't earned it, but I never thought heaven could be so . . . tactile."

He was feeling the silk sheets of his bed, but he was looking at the girl.

"You're not dead, Mr Klein," she replied, "but in a sense you might say you've gone to heaven."

Simon looked past her out the open window of his spacious room at the wide lawn and brilliantly flowering garden beyond.

"Looks more like Sussex than heaven," he said. "I hate to be so unoriginal, but where am I?"

"You'll hear all about that in a minute. I'm not supposed to discuss anything except your comfort and pleasure with you."

The Saint nodded.

"You're a specialist, then, I take it."

She gave him a dazzling smile.

"I hope so. Are you comfortable?"

"Supremely."

"Do your pyjamas fit?" she asked. "I had to guess the size."

"A perfect guess, Miss . . ."

"You can call me Galaxy."

"Galaxy? As in Milky Way?"

"Of course. Galaxy Rose. From your novel, remember? *Volcano Seven.*"

She turned towards the closed door on Simon's left as he sat in bed.

"Wait," he said. "I'd like to . . ."

"Oh, I'm not leaving you, Mr Klein. I'm here to serve you . . . with anything you want."

She opened the door and drew in a wheeled table laid with white linen, crystal, and silver serving dishes. There was a single rose in a slender vase. Simon, at the sight of the breakfast, discovered that his appetite had not been hurt in the least by whatever had happened during the night. He got out of bed, Galaxy helped him into a robe, and he took a seat at the table.

"Comfy?" she asked, pouring his coffee.

"Absolutely."

"The London papers," she said.

Simon put the newspapers aside and applied himself to the coffee.

"Very thoughtful, but I don't think the news I'm interested in would be in the papers."

"What news? If you're thinking of your . . . ah . . . friend, or secretary, or whatever she is, she's in the room next door. She's still asleep, and she's fine."

"I'm glad to hear that. And secondly, then, I'd like to know whether you've kidnapped us or rescued us. In either case I can't say I'm terribly unhappy at the moment, but it might affect my long-range view of things."

Galaxy Rose was serving him honeydew melon in its nest of ice.

"I hope you like melon," she said. "From now on you can order anything, but this time I had to do it for you."

"That's great, but back to my question . . ."

"You're in a private house, in the country," the girl said evasively.

"Whose private house?"

She looked at her watch.

"For that information, you'll have to wait thirty seconds. I already told you I can't answer those kind of questions. Would you like a bath or shower before you get dressed?"

"Shower. What happens in thirty seconds?"

"Look up there."

She pointed to a wooden panel on the wall to the right, on the opposite side of the room from the door through which she had brought Simon's breakfast.

"Fascinating," he said.

"You'll see," she told him. "I'll go see that everything's ready for your shower when you've finished."

She left through a door next to the wooden panel. The instant she was out of sight, Simon started to get to his feet, but at the same time an almost imperceptible buzzing sound called his attention back to the panel. It was sliding up, revealing a television screen that flickered with featureless light. Then the face of a man appeared. He was a plump man, and he looked absolutely delighted with himself and the world. He was staring directly at Simon, smiling broadly.

"Good morning, Mr Klein, and welcome!" he boomed.

His countenance produced inevitable thoughts of Mr Pickwick, the Wizard of Oz, and Father Christmas. At the same time, there was something small and piggish and strange about the opaque darkness of his eyes. He was also capable of producing recollections of such mad and unsavoury gentlemen as certain Roman emperors who were given to killing their friends and relatives in moments of pique, and whose delusions knew no bounds.

He licked his thick lips and went on: "Firstly, I must apologize for my rather forceful method of bringing you here, but when it became obvious that you were not going to cash my cheque, I had to force the issue." He paused for effect. "Yes, Mr Klein . . . I am Warlock."

Judging from the intensity with which the man who called himself Warlock seemed to be looking at him, Simon decided that he actually could be seen. There was undoubtedly a television camera—probably more than one—scanning the room in which he was being served such a well-prepared breakfast. He went back to enjoying it, waving a piece of toast at Warlock's image in cheerful salutation.

"No doubt you are wondering what this is all about," the speaker continued. "I shall explain only briefly now, for we shall have ample opportunity to discuss details in the days to come."

Warlock clasped his hands, took a happy sigh, and looked very much like a man about to distribute toys to a roomful of orphans . . . or like Caligula, with a laurel crown of thinning hair rimming his bald head, about to set in motion some monstrous battle between Christians and crocodiles.

"This is your imagination brought to reality," he said, extending an upturned palm on either side. "I've long admired your books. They've given me more pleasure and stimulated more dreams than you would ever have believed if you had never come here. Yes, I am Warlock, and you are in the headquarters of SWORD. Everything is exactly as you described it in your books. Not one detail is missing . . . though I must flatter myself in telling you that in transforming an author's fantasies into reality, however thorough and brilliant the author may be—as you most certainly are, Mr Klein—one nevertheless discovers that some details have been overlooked in the books and must be supplied by the practical man."

The Saint nodded understandingly towards the screen and went to work on his eggs and bacon. Warlock sat back in his chair and beamed.

"I know you'll understand that no criticism is intended," he went on. "I'm only pointing out an inevitable difference between literature and life. But far be it from me to pretend to be a literary critic. I am a simple and wholehearted admirer of the creative imagination, with only amateurish pretensions in that direction myself. A few poems here and there—childish things really, not worth your trouble, but of course if you should have time to glance at them and give me your honest . . ." Warlock, who obviously had a tendency to become hypnotized by the sound of his own voice, waved a disparaging hand. "But I'm wandering. You are the creative genius, and I am the practical man. One might compare our relationship to that of Voltaire and Frederick the Great, or Michelangelo and the Medici . . . But again I'm getting ahead of myself. You had a trying night, Mr Klein. Please finish your breakfast at your leisure, bathe if you wish, and when you're quite ready, please join us in the planning room. I'll explain everything there. Galaxy— one of your more delightful creations, I must say—will show you the way. In the meantime, if there's anything we've overlooked, or if there's anything you want, you have only to ask her. Anything at all. Welcome again, Mr Klein, and good-bye for now."

The screen went dark, and the wooden panel slid quietly back across it.

"You hear that, Galaxy?" Simon called. "Anything I want, I've only to ask."

"I heard," said Galaxy.

She emerged eagerly from the bathroom and Simon met her hazel eyes with the magnetic power of his startling blue ones.

"Anything," he repeated wickedly.

Galaxy came towards him.

"What did you have in mind?" she asked softly.

"A gun."

Her lips were suddenly compressed with irritation.

"What a shame," she said. "Some people don't know when they have it good."

Simon sipped his coffee.

"You realize that if you don't give me a gun you're making Mr Warlock guilty of false advertising. And if this pleasure palace is all as dandy as you people seem to think it is, what harm could a little automatic do? I happen to like playing with guns, and if we're all here to play I can't see why we can't play some games I like."

Even Galaxy's modest brain could distinguish between teasing and seriousness. She stopped pouting and smiled as quickly as the sun might pop out from behind a passing summer cloud.

"You're sweet," she said, "but I can't give you a gun. I've already fetched your breakfast, tested your shower, and I'm about to lay out your clothes and anything else you want, so why can't you just be co-operative?"

"I think I might like it if you called me master," he said. "As long as I've got a slave, I might as well enjoy every last tingle."

Galaxy laughed.

"All right, master."

Simon got to his feet, touched his lips with his napkin, and dropped the cloth on the table. He put a strong hand on each of her shoulders.

"So now, lovely slave, how about getting me a gun? All I want it for is to defend us against the blokes who'll be trying to shoot their way in here . . . to get at you."

Her smile faded and her lips parted. Her eyes seemed to grow smoky with anticipation as he leaned near her.

"I can't," she breathed.

Simon threw up his hands and turned towards the bathroom.

"Then put me out a clean shirt and a blue suit, would you?" he said matter-of-factly.

Galaxy clenched her fists.

"You—"

Simon lounged at the bathroom door, pointing up at the panel which covered the television screen.

"Naughty," he said. "Remember, you're my willing slave, and you'll learn that as long as my every whim is satisfied instantly I'm absolutely super to get along with."

Once more the cloud passed and she laughed.

"Very good, master. You run along and take your shower, and I'll come scrub your back. My orders are to conserve your energy."

"You're too generous."

"I've hardly even started."

4

Forty-five minutes later, the Saint stood before a full-length mirror and studied the fit of his blue trousers and white shirt.

"You must give me the name of Mr Warlock's tailor," he said, "so I can avoid him."

"They fit quite well," Galaxy said. "Not knowing what you were like, we had to get it all different sizes. And now you complain!"

"A fit is not just a matter of clothes falling somewhere between too large and too small. It's a product of art. Mr Warlock would understand that. He has an aesthetic soul."

"Well," Galaxy replied, giving his shirt a playful but vicious tug, "I didn't choose the clothes. What else can I do for you?"

Simon thought.

"I feel mean this morning. How about a . . . a blue tie with purple spots?"

"Immediately, master," said Galaxy.

A moment later she returned from the wardrobe with a blue tie infected with spots so gorgeously purple as to make a grape turn raisin with envy. Simon sighed and knotted it around his neck.

"Okay, Friday, you win. Let's get on to the confrontation."

Galaxy Rose held Simon's jacket for him, and led him to the door of his room. Her hand caught his wrist as he started to turn the burnished steel knob.

"You should know better than that," she said. "Or do you like the sound of loud bells?"

The Saint's memory ranged back over the Charles Lake adventures he had read.

"Electronic locks," he said, "controlled from a central station. But don't tell me you have the fingerprint scanning device."

"Of course we do."

Simon was impressed.

"But it doesn't really exist," he argued. "I just made it up."

"It exists now," Galaxy told him. "Warlock says that one of the beauties of your imagination is that the things you come up with almost always really would work, if only somebody took the trouble to make them."

She pointed to a small, faintly glowing translucent disc set into the wall beside the door handle. She pressed her thumb against it for two seconds, while supposedly (Simon was not entirely convinced that the system was genuine) a photo-electric cell scanned the thumbprint and transmitted its pattern to the memory bank of a central computer which made its recognition and signalled approval by electrically unlocking the door.

"Warlock is very thorough," said the Saint.

There was a light *ping* as the lock was disengaged. He turned the handle without producing a fusillade of alarm bells, and Galaxy Rose preceded him into the hallway.

"This way to the stairs," she said.

The hall, simply carpeted and devoid of furnishings, had none of the luxury-hotel quality that had characterized the Saint's room. Except for the carpet, it reminded him of the spotlessly clean and purely utilitarian companionway of a ship. He could imagine the exotic gadgets which might reside behind some of the metal panels in the white walls. And the circular grids in the ceiling probably protected more interesting devices than mere electric light bulbs. There were numbered doors at intervals on either side of the corridor; all were closed.

Simon, still a little dazed by the sheer implausibility of everything that had happened to him, was somewhat like a man in a dream who is telling himself that he's only dreaming and that he must wake up. He wanted to maintain his scepticism, to remind himself that the statements he had heard made about this building and its occupants were too far-fetched to believe. Yet he had been given evidence that the claims had at least some foundation to them. For the time being he could only go along with the gag, keep himself ready for anything, and hope that his future experiences with the Secret World Organization for Retribution and Destruction would be even a fraction as pleasant as his room, his breakfast, and Galaxy Rose.

The corridor opened on to the landing of a wide staircase which led down to a large living room furnished eighteenth-century style, enriched with armour, landscape paintings, and neo-classic sculpture. The room was in no way particularly different from the main reception room of any other English country mansion, except for one thing: he had the unsettling experience of deja vu, as if he knew the place intimately and yet at the same time knew that he had never been there. Then he realized the reason for the sensation: the room had been described in Amos Klein's books, and the designer of the room in which Simon now stood had gone to great pains to duplicate every detail.

Galaxy was watching her charge's reactions, half-smiling at his bemusement.

"Something wrong?" she asked.

"No. It's just that everything's too right. It's a little hard to believe."

"It is, isn't it?" Galaxy said cheerfully. For a split second the cloud shadow that Simon had noticed before crossed her face, but her voice betrayed nothing. "I had a hard time believing it myself for a while."

As he followed her down the long room towards closed doors of heavy oak, he was more fascinated than ever by the operations of his own mind in these strange circumstances. His powers of recall had always been exceptional and had more than a few times brought him success or even saved his life because of the advantage they gave him. But when he had read the Charles Lake books he had done so entirely for entertainment, or even derision, and with no thought at all that there would be any point In remembering even details of the plots, much less the names of characters, the descriptions of rooms, or the mechanisms of the fantastic devices so prevalent in Charles Lake's weird world.

But now Simon had new confirmation of something he had always believed—that nothing in one's experience was ever really lost, though the calling up to consciousness of long "forgotten" facts seemed more responsive to accidental association than to a deliberate effort of will. The stimulus of the Saint's surroundings—the names, the gadgets, the furnishings—began to revive more and more details of the Amos Klein novels he had read. At first the trickle of recollections had been small, but now the revelations came like the rapid thawing of tributaries in the spring—streams flowing into larger brooks, brooks flowing into rivers. Now Simon's mind was filling with a torrent of facts about the world of Charles Lake which was astonishing in its completeness.

As Amos Klein—a role that had been thrust upon him, and which he welcomed in the circumstances—he had to know those things about the novels he had supposedly written. He was grateful to the mental gift which renewed a knowledge that he might reasonably have expected to have lost forever.

"Here we are," Galaxy said.

They were standing in front of another pair of oaken doors, but before she could expose her thumb to the glowing yellow disc beside them, they swung open from within, revealing what Warlock called the planning room.

"Greetings, Mr Klein, and welcome to your rightful place in the world."

The speaker was Warlock himself. He stood just a few feet inside the doorway, and even in his immaculate grey suit he managed to look like a jovial Caligula. The room which provided the setting for his welcome was large, richly panelled with oak, and strikingly modern in contrast to the room Simon was leaving. Behind the expansive Warlock was a long mahogany table. Around the table stood four men, two of whom the Saint recognized immediately as the phoney policemen of the night before.

"Overwhelmed," said the Saint, inclining slightly.

Warlock did not miss the mocking twist of Simon's lips. He nodded approvingly.

"So far, Mr Klein, you have lived up to my fondest expectations. I might have known you'd take all this with the same aplomb as Charles Lake . . . although of course I had no way of telling whether or not you'd resemble him in the slightest."

Warlock spoke precisely, with a neutral British accent which told nothing about him except that he had probably artificially cultivated his present way of speaking—in the same way that a radio announcer or actor tends to lose the speech patterns of his native region. Warlock's accent, as a matter of fact, resembled that of the actor who played the role of Warlock in the Charles Lake films.

"We're always told," he continued, "that one should never meet one's favourite author. The man might be so much less impressive than his work that one could be terribly disappointed. But I must say, Mr

Klein, that I'm not disappointed at all. I'm delighted! You're much more Charles Lake than the man who plays his part in the films."

Simon bowed his thanks.

"I hope I'll be half as delighted when I find out why you gassed and kidnapped me."

Warlock looked hurt. His jowls sagged.

"I wish you wouldn't look at it that way, Mr Klein. It seemed to me that since you were understandably dubious about my original offer, I must use unorthodox methods . . . for the good of both of us. I trust you'll soon forgive me when you hear my plan."

"I don't have much choice at the moment," said the Saint.

Warlock gave a deprecating wave of his hand, as if pretending not even to hear such an unworthy remark.

"Now, Mr Klein, please come in, won't you? This is your planning room. You'll recognize it, of course."

Simon accompanied Warlock across the thick carpet, glancing at the beamed ceiling, the high windows which allowed a view only of the sky, and the walls lined with books, maps, and graphs.

"I do recognize it," Simon said. He had decided to bring a little more of the overawed author into his characterization. "It's hard to believe. A perfect replica of the SWORD planning room."

Warlock rubbed his hands delightedly.

"Not a replica," he said. "This is the SWORD planning room— the only one on earth. Not in your mind, not on paper, not on film, but here, in reality!"

"And you've done all this yourselves?" Simon asked.

"I have done it," Warlock said. "These gentlemen by the table were chosen after the building was completed. It has been absolutely guaranteed that my interests are theirs. Their loyalty is beyond question. You'll recognize them, I think? You created them."

Warlock stood happily by while Simon inspected the troops, who stood in varying postures of respectful unease on either side of the table.

"Bishop," Simon said to the one who had come to the cottage door as P. C. Jarvis.

Bishop, whose chin displayed a dark bruise where Simon had hit him, forced a smile. He was no longer in uniform but like the other men wore a conservatively tailored suit.

"Mr Klein," he said politely, by way of acknowledgement.

"Feeling chipper this morning, Bishop? That's good."

Simon moved on to the giant who had accompanied Bishop in the impersonation of police constables.

"Simeon Monk, as I live and breathe. Do you really bend railroad irons with your bare hands?"

"Yes," said Simeon Monk succinctly.

"Better have that throat looked after, Sim. Sounds as if you're talking from down in a barrel."

Simeon rubbed his throat and looked confused.

"He always sounds that way," Warlock explained unnecessarily. "Remember, in *Volcano Seven*, you described . . ."

"Right," the Saint agreed. "He's perfect. And this handsome fellow here will be . . . don't tell me, let me guess . . . Frug!"

The word "handsome" had probably never been applied to Frug before, even as a joke. He would have been more aptly described, by a speaker less sardonic and more brutally honest than the Saint chose to be at the moment, as an ugly little shrimp. Opposite the huge Neanderthal called Monk, he looked even shorter and more shrimpy than he was, the perfect caricature of the chain smoker who spends his afternoons at the racetrack and his evenings in a billiards hall.

"Pleased to make your acquaintance," Frug said deferentially.

"And who is this?" Simon asked. "As if I didn't know."

He was inspecting the last member of the quartet, a moderately tall man of almost albino colouration. His hair was white, he seemed to have no eyebrows, and his eyes themselves were the palest of milky grey. He seemed to have more difficulty looking either cordial or respectful than any of the others.

"Nero Jones," he said.

The Saint turned back to Warlock.

"At least I can't find fault with the casting," he remarked.

"I am so pleased you think so," Warlock replied. "I do think our group here is much more true to life"—he laughed and interrupted himself—"I should say, true to fiction, to your books, than the cast in the motion pictures. I want you to understand that from the very beginning I've tried to depend on your books entirely and to ignore the films, so as to be as faithful as possible to your own ideas. I can't deny being influenced by the films, but I've tried not to be unduly influenced. It was your ideas I was interested in, and a lot of other writers messing about with them could easily spoil the whole thing."

"What whole thing?" Simon asked impatiently.

"I don't blame you for being puzzled," Warlock answered. "Here. Please. Sit down at the head of the table, the place of honour, the place of the leader. I'll explain everything."

He ushered Simon to the high-backed chair. Galaxy remained decoratively in the doorway.

"You may go now, Galaxy," Warlock said. "Mr Klein won't need you for a while, will you, Mr Klein?"

"Not for the next minute or so, anyway," Simon said fondly.

"Good," Warlock continued. "Galaxy, go see that Mr Klein's . . . er . . . acquaintance is being well taken care of."

Galaxy left, closing the double doors behind her, and Warlock looked at Simon.

"The lady is your . . ." He paused, questioningly.

"Associate," Simon said, with a vagueness he thought should cover any story Amity Little might have come up with.

Warlock produced the knowing smile of a man who did not really know much about such things but wanted the world to think he did.

"Understood, Mr Klein, understood. And now, let's get down to business, shall we?"

"Fine," the Saint said bluntly. "I'm a prisoner, is that the idea?"

Warlock looked mildly pained.

"Only in the most technical sense of the word," he said. "You were brought here involuntarily, true, but I'm sure that when you hear my plan you'll be very happy that you came. Remember, Mr Klein, you are the leader. You are the father. We are your brain children."

The Saint sat back in his chair and surveyed the other men—Warlock facing him from the other end of the table, the others seated along either side.

"And what do I do? Play cops and robbers with you children in this gigantic dollhouse? I feel as if it and all of us were cut off the back of a box of breakfast cereal."

For the first time the man who called himself Warlock lost his composure. It was only a momentary loss, but it showed the ugly strength which lay behind the jovial surface. Veins bulged and pulsed at his temples, and his black eyes seemed distended in their sockets. But self-control was re-established in a few seconds. His face recovered its normal flaccid pallor as his blood subsided.

"Mr Klein," he said softly, "this is no child's game. It is not a joke. All this has been done for a practical purpose—a most eminently practical purpose: the purpose of making money. What I have done here is build a business organization and a headquarters for that business. The business is called SWORD and it was conceived by you as well as christened by you. I have made it a reality for the simple reason that it works."

Simon looked soberly at Warlock.

"You mean you've planned to put an organization like SWORD into actual operation?"

Warlock leaned forward.

"SWORD is in operation," he said. "It was quite efficient in bringing you here. The Secret World Organization for Retribution and Destruction is no longer just a fiction. It exists."

"And Warlock has come to life to be its boss," Simon said.

Warlock sat back in his chair, looking pleased with himself once more.

"Oh, no, Mr Klein. I'm not the boss. You are. The ingredient that makes SWORD unique is the unique brain of a creative genius—your own remarkable brain. Without that, SWORD would be only a body without life, a machine without fuel, a . . . a weapon without a finger to pull the trigger."

"Before you drown us with metaphors, Mr X, let me be sure I understand the facts; you've kidnapped me so that I can be the badly needed brain behind this organization. Together, I take it, we're going to become multi-billionaires, put the Mafia out of business by beating it at its own game, and even manipulate governments from behind the scenes—small governments at first, and then work our way up to the really big ones until we control the world."

Warlock's eyes glowed like cinders under a bellows.

"You do understand, Mr Klein! I knew you would. Nero! The attaché case."

The near-albino rose from his chair and went to fetch the case from a table behind him.

"This will help convince you of our sincerity," Warlock continued. "Once you come to trust me, I'm sure you'll agree that a life of real action, a life in which one lives his art rather than merely dreaming it—I'm sure you'll agree that such a life and its rewards are far preferable to fiction and fantasies."

"But not necessarily more profitable," Simon said.

"This should convince you even more. Nero, if you please."

Nero set the attaché case on the table in front of the Saint and unlocked it. Simon opened it himself. Inside were tightly bound stacks of ten-pound notes.

"That's certainly quite an argument," the Saint admitted.

He had decided that his best tactic was to play along, for the moment, until he found out just how far Warlock's well-heeled madness would go. He tried to look like an author who, even though rich from his writing, was not above being impressed by such quantities of money.

"And that's only half," Warlock told him. "Fifty thousand pounds. Remember my offer in the post? Fifty thousand now and another fifty thousand after two months, at the successful conclusion of our first major project."

Simon Templar tried to look as flattered, intrigued, and seriously tempted as an imaginary Amos Klein might have looked.

"What might that be?" he asked. "This major project."

"We are going . . ." Warlock began, and then he paused for effect as he put his hand on the table and took a deep breath. "We are going to rob the largest storehouse of treasure on this side of the Atlantic. We are going to empty it of gold, platinum, and diamonds worth more millions of pounds than I can ever estimate."

"We are?" Simon asked solemnly, building up his part.

"We are," Warlock said. "And your brain is going to tell us how it can be done."

"Do you think I could? Even if I . . ."

"I know you can," Warlock said flatly. "I know you will."

"All right," said the Saint. "Where is this king-size piggy bank?"

CHAPTER THREE:

HOW WARLOCK MADE HIS PITCH AND SIMON TEMPLAR TOOK A WALK

1

"It's called Hermetico," Warlock said. "Have you heard of it?"

"No," Simon lied.

He knew of the existence of the place, but until now he had taken no special interest in it. He relaxed in his chair as Warlock took charge of a small table draped with purple velvet which had been rolled over next to the long conference table. Out of the corner of his eye Simon noted the strained, attentive faces of the other men. Their tension made for interesting speculation. Had Warlock, who apparently had money in large supply, not only gained their loyalty by paying them plenty, but possibly by recruiting them from prisons whose wardens had viewed the men's departure with surprise and alarm rather than that warm satisfaction which comes of seeing the regenerate and rehabilitated outlaw leave for a better life at the end of a fully served term? If that were the case, then well-justified fear, if not gratitude, would considerably enhance their devotion to SWORD and its leader.

"This is a model of Hermetico," Warlock said.

Frug, the more skimpy but most intelligent-looking of Warlock's minions, lifted the purple covering from the table, revealing a monolithic white building surrounded by fences.

"There's not much to it, is there?" Simon remarked nonchalantly.

"It's like an iceberg," Warlock answered. "Only the least important part shows above the surface. Hermetico was formerly the Templedown Colliery in North Wales, and now—"

"You've had it moved down to your property for a fish pond," the Saint interrupted pleasantly.

Warlock darted him a look which did not say much for Warlock's sense of humour. Simon looked repentant.

"I just meant," he explained, "that you seem to be able to work miracles, so I wouldn't be surprised at anything you've done now."

Warlock was somewhat appeased, though still suspicious.

"The Templedown Colliery," he continued, "was bought by a private company who have converted it into an underground depository for hyper-valuables."

"Hyper-valuables?" Simon asked innocently. "What are hyper-valuables?"

Warlock turned impatiently from his model.

"Hyper-valuables are . . . very valuable things. I got the word from one of your books."

"Oh," Simon said, embarrassed. "Well, even Homer nods."

"For example, two of the Middle East countries store their gold reserves there."

"One of them keeps its crown jewels there," Frug volunteered.

Warlock nodded.

"And three of De Beers's subsidiaries keep diamond stocks there," he said.

"And Oppenheimer's, too," said Frug.

By now everybody in the room was looking at the white model building as if it itself were made of diamonds. Warlock reverently touched its domed roof.

"So you can see, Mr Klein, that it's a worthy target for your talents."

Simon stood with his hands clasped behind him and looked down at the model treasure-house.

"There's just one thing wrong for a start," he said.

"What's that?" Warlock asked.

"Where does Charles Lake come in? He's my hero, remember? He's supposed to keep people from doing things like this, not cheer them on while they steal some poor potentate's family jewels."

Warlock was not taken aback.

"I could not create Charles Lake even if I wanted to. One cannot create an individual, but one can create an organization. And having created this organization, and all the resources and equipment with which your imagination endowed it on paper, I can only be glad that there is no such person as a Charles Lake in the real world." Warlock's small mouth smiled faintly, a dark crevasse in the snowy hills of his face. "SWORD actually exists. Charles Lake does not. And there's your answer, Mr Klein. If you're worried about the moral considerations, let's discuss those later."

"All right," said Simon. He nodded towards the model. "Go ahead, please. I'm interested in the problem of cracking this place . . . just in theory, of course."

Warlock gave him a delighted glance and put his hand once more on the white dome of the little building.

"The surface structure is bomb-proof. Conventional bombs, I mean. Only the subterranean levels are proof against atomic bombs, and it's at those levels, far below the ground, that the valuables are stored." Warlock's stubby finger touched the fence which surrounded the building. "Twelve feet high, barbed, and every strand wired to the alarm system. Between the fence and the narrow walkway surrounding the building there's an area crisscrossed with electromagnetic beams. If one of the beams is interrupted an alarm goes off and a buried mine explodes at the point at which the beam was broken."

The Saint bent over the model.

"Sounds formidable enough," he commented.

"The place is supposed to be absolutely theft-proof," Warlock said proudly.

"Maybe we could start with something easy," the Saint said. "Like the Bank of England."

"I'm glad you've learned to say 'we' so quickly," Warlock responded. "I can see that you find the project interesting."

Simon had used the "we" as an ocean fisherman uses bits of chopped fish to attract and put his prey off guard before he drops his hook. Having decided that his best strategy was to pretend to be tempted by Warlock's proposition, he might as well stay on that tack. For the moment there was nothing to be gained by resisting, and there might be a great deal to be learned by ostensibly co-operating.

"It's interesting," he said. "And challenging."

Warlock turned the table around, showing that the underground sections of Hermetico had also been incorporated into the model, extending below tabletop level. He removed half of the surface model, so that now a complete cross-section view of the Hermetico complex was visible—the low building at ground level, the narrow vertical shaft, and the spreading chambers, like the roots of a tree, at the bottom.

"In the surface building," Warlock said, "are business offices, switchboard, and controls for the surface security complex." His fingers followed the long shaft downwards. "Here, an elevator, of course, and near the lower mouth of the shaft, the central control room. There are grilles of steel bars at intervals throughout the storage area, each with a different locking system and automatic sealing device. In the event of an alarm, the whole storage area can be flooded. The whole thing is automated."

Bishop, the constable of the night before, had been standing respectfully by.

"Not the friendliest place in the world," he volunteered chattily.

Warlock gave him a chilling glance as Simon straightened up after a close inspection of the lower chambers.

"Automated?" he asked. "You mean there aren't any guards?"

"Oh, I'm afraid there are, but not nearly as many as you might expect. They serve a caretaking purpose, primarily. The management of Hermetico apparently feel that their automatic mechanical devices are more than adequate to discourage any attempt at theft."

"And so the battle was lost . . ." Simon murmured.

"What's that?" Warlock asked.

"It's that kind of feeling that loses battles," Simon said.

Warlock cast jubilant glances at his staff.

"So you see a loophole already!" he exclaimed to the Saint. "You can do it!"

Simon managed to look blankly innocent.

"I?" he said. "I only meant that over-confidence can make the most perfect defences vulnerable."

"Then you will find that weak point," Warlock replied. "The basic idea came to me from your book, *Volcano Seven*, except there it was the Bank of England SWORD robbed."

"Tried to rob," Simon corrected him. "Charles Lake stopped them."

"And of course that's one of the beauties of having you on SWORD's side, Mr Klein!" Warlock crowed. "You'll come up with an even better story this time, in which SWORD wins."

Simon elaborated his blank innocence into confusion.

"Story?" he asked.

"Telling how SWORD ransacked Hermetico. How through brilliant thinking, they breached every defence, penetrated to the core of that invulnerable fortress, and left it bare!"

"I'm to do that," Simon marvelled rather than asked. "That's the literary project you sent me that fifty-thousand-pound retainer for."

Warlock rubbed his hands gleefully. He was pacing up and down the rich carpet near the model of Hermetico. The pale faces of his henchmen followed his movements like the spectators of a tennis match.

"Of course," he said. "But it's much more than a literary project. Here's your opportunity to live your art and bring your wildest dreams to reality."

"Bring your wildest dreams to reality," Simon said drily. "Mine were doing fine already."

Warlock stopped his peregrinations.

"I think," he said, "that we might continue this discussion in private. You've met your staff, so to speak, and I see no point in keeping them here, if you agree."

"I see no point in it at all," Simon said.

"Very well, gentlemen, you may go. Except, Frug, would you please leave us the Hermetico dossier?" Warlock turned to Simon. "This dossier Frug will give you contains complete details of Hermetico operations and layout, including blue-prints. Frug?"

Frug, who had been looking quite pleased with himself during most of the meeting, jerked slightly and demonstrated that the skin of a more or less living human being, however white it may be, can always turn a little whiter.

"I don't have it," he blurted. "I mean, it's in my office. I'll just be a minute."

Frug sidled towards the doorway, but Warlock stopped him with a word. It was a softly spoken word, with all the gentle menace of an adder sliding towards its sleeping prey.

"Frug."

"Yes," Frug said. "Yes, sir?"

Warlock confronted him, the jowly face, blotched with anger, threatening the scrawny white one.

"I told you to bring it, Frug," Warlock said quietly.

"I forgot. I . . ."

With an awkwardly prolonged movement whose implications Frug could clearly see, Warlock drew back his right arm and brought it across in a sweeping arc that smashed flat-handed on the side of Frug's pointed face. The Saint, whose first reaction to Frug had been a strong but entirely impersonal impulse to pop him like an insect between the earth and the sole of his shoe, viewed the performance with gratification and interest. It interested him that Frug had not tried to avoid the blow he saw coming, and that after it knocked his head to one side with its force, Frug did not betray by so much of a glint in his narrow eyes the rage that he must feel. Warlock's power, then, was built on a sound foundation. His organization was not going to fall apart just because it was new and based on a mad dream.

"SWORD cannot afford members who forget," Warlock said. "Since this is your first error, we'll overlook it. Take the dossier to Mr Klein's room after he has returned there."

Warlock looked at his other men, who had not moved during Frug's punishment.

"You gentlemen may go now. See that Mr Klein has the typewriter and other materials." Warlock, his face still mottled crimson as an aftermath of his outburst, turned to his captive author, and the corners of his small mouth curved smugly upwards in one of the most unsavoury smiles the Saint had ever seen on a human countenance. "Then be sure you don't disturb him," he concluded. "He'll be a very busy fellow for the next few days."

2

"And what if I refuse?" Simon asked when he and Warlock were alone in the oak-panelled planning room.

Warlock turned from the double doors which he had closed securely behind his departing staff. Simon was standing entirely at ease near the model of Hermetico. Warlock came towards him, stopped, raised his arms from his sides, and then dropped them with a heavy sigh.

"Why must you put me in an awkward position by asking such a question, Mr Klein? Why must you be difficult when I've gone to such lengths to prove my competence and my real interest in your work?" He made a gesture that encompassed the whole building around him. "What greater compliment could an author have than that a man of science, a practical businessman—"

"A scholar and a gentleman?" queried the Saint.

Warlock ignored the interruption except to re-adjust his sentence. "—that I should want to bring your fiction to reality? What could be more exciting? The masses read your works and forget them. I want to bring your energies to bear on the material world, to make you the architect of great feats, conquests . . ."

Warlock had begun to pace the room, waving his arms and working himself into a literal lather. Simon interrupted him quietly.

"Yes, but what happens if I don't want to do it?" he asked.

Warlock stopped and sighed more heavily than ever.

"Must you, Mr Klein? Must we discuss such unpleasant possibilities? Can't you feel yourself infected with the same excitement that moves me so profoundly?"

Simon put his hands in his pockets and walked slowly to the wall beneath one of the high windows.

"I can feel myself infected, all right, but I can also see myself locked up in one of Her Majesty's free boarding houses if this scheme of yours falls through."

Warlock, sensing a weakening of resistance, all but scampered to confront the Saint and eagerly grasped his arms.

"Not my scheme," he said, his jowls aquiver, "your scheme! Don't you see—I want you to want to do this. I have no desire to force you."

"Then I'm free to go whenever I feel like it?"

Warlock loosened his grip and started to speak, then was silent. He paced away, then paced back, started to speak again, and ended up beside the Hermetico model. His hand touched the white-domed top of the surface building. He stared down at it as if it were a crystal ball in which he could see visions.

"Mr Klein," he said softly, "when I was a lad, I was a dreamer. I read more than most because at that time I suffered from an illness that kept me from taking part in outdoor games like the other boys. My mind was full of adventures, and explorations, and the lives of great men. I imagined myself with Alexander in Persia, with Drake on the Spanish Main, and with Livingstone in Africa, but I wasn't content just to imagine. I wanted to live those adventures."

He paused, his hand slipping from the model on the tabletop. Simon stood without moving. He wanted to do nothing that might discourage his captor from going on with his personal confessions.

"I remember a curious kind of incident," Warlock continued. "It illustrates what I mean. One night I was playing on the carpet with some lead soldiers my father had brought me. I asked him—my father—to play with me, and actually I was very surprised when he did, but he got down on his knees and we spent a long time arranging the soldiers on opposing sides. We had cannon and cavalry and infantry, and we made hills of blankets and cushions, and walls of books, and rivers and trees of paper and such . . . and when it was all done it looked quite impressive, the two armies ready for attack, poised on the hills and in the woods, ready to fire, ready to charge. And my father said, 'Well, now, that's fine,' and got up and began to read his paper again. And I began crying, and he looked down and said, 'Now, good heavens, what's the matter? Didn't I play with you?' And I went on blubbering and said, 'But they don't do anything. They don't move.' It was strange." Warlock shook his head. "I don't even know why it upset me so much. I cried as if my heart was broken."

Simon felt more embarrassed than enlightened by the story. He merely shrugged slightly and allowed Warlock a new span of encouraging silence.

"The point is, Mr Klein, that it is very difficult and rare to find opportunities for heroism and grand actions these days. I went to work for the research branch of an electronics firm after I'd finished at the university. That, at least, seemed an opportunity to explore new fields, if only in the mind. But the whole endeavour was smothered under a great weight of bureaucracy and practical necessity and professional jealousy." Warlock folded his hands behind him and began to pace again. "I decided to launch out on my own. Frankly, I stole. I falsified requisitions and forged signatures. I had very little money, but over months I managed to build up a quite respectable laboratory in my cottage outside town. And then, before I was even certain what direction I'd take, two wonderful things happened to me: I discovered your books and I inherited this estate and four hundred thousand pounds."

Simon acknowledged Amos Klein's admiration of the sum.

"I'm flattered that you'd even include my books in the same sentence," he said.

Warlock was so engrossed in his own words that he did not even glance at the Saint.

"Your books," he said, "and others like them, are the healthy dreams of a sick humanity. People are stifled by an age in which aggressive instincts are held up to shame and scorn, when the invisible powers of money rule everything, when machines and taxes and collectivist politics destroy initiative and offer no challenge to self-development! Only in books like yours can they find a breath of fresh air and a glimpse of a way of life in which men use themselves to the full."

"Hear, hear!" Simon applauded. "And you're going to solve the problem by robbing safe deposits?"

Even though the Saint's tone was kept carefully free of heavy sarcasm, anger flared across Warlock's face like a sudden bruise.

"I'm sorry you don't understand me!" he snapped. "It isn't often I would bare my feelings to anyone, but I thought that you, of all people, would . . ."

Warlock bogged down.

"Sympathize?" the Saint offered. This time he spoke in a more friendly way than before, projecting an Amos Klein who was intrigued and tempted but torn by distrust and fear which he desperately wanted to hide. "Maybe I do sympathize, more than you know, but with four hundred thousand quid in the bank, why do you want to steal?"

"I chose to regard that inheritance merely as starting capital. It is, as the Americans say, peanuts—compared with the wealth of men like Onassis, Hughes, or Getty. I intend to have as much as they have— and more. I don't care what I invest in this first operation: it will be returned hundreds of times. And those millions in turn will finance still greater operations. I see no limit to what may be mine one day. And you can be my partner."

"Fine," said the Saint. "But can you blame me for being cautious? After all, I've been gassed, kidnapped, and now told I'm to devise a way of pulling off the most spectacular and dangerous robbery in history. Am I supposed to feel perfectly calm?"

Warlock began to exude hopefulness again as he and Simon faced one another over the model of Hermetico.

"But I've apologized for kidnapping you," he said, as if he sincerely believed that ought to be enough for anybody. "And there's the fifty thousand pounds just as an advance on the Hermetico profits—and there's fine food, and people to wait on you hand and foot, and every comfort, and Galaxy Rose, and—"

Simon held up his hand.

"Nobody could complain about the accommodations," he said. "Especially not about Galaxy Rose. But no matter how pleasant it all is, I'm bothered by the nagging feeling that I'm a prisoner. When do I get to spend some of that fifty thousand? If I agreed to co-operate with you on this project, am I and my . . . associate free to come and go as we please?"

Warlock shook his head apologetically.

"I'm afraid, Mr Klein, that that must wait until I can be quite sure of your loyalty—or until you are as deeply compromised as the rest of us."

"Which is just a polite way of saying that I am a prisoner?"

"If you agree to stay here voluntarily, then you needn't think of yourself as a prisoner."

"And if I don't agree?"

Warlock struggled not to lose his temper completely over this new relapse.

"If you insist on being difficult, on pushing me into that position, the answer is that you have no choice. You are going to work with me as I planned. You've supplied me, if it comes to the worst, with too many gruesome methods of torture to make refusal even thinkable, particularly since I'd let Nero and Monk practise on the girl before they started on you. I think they'd hardly be warmed up before you'd be begging them to let her go and give you a typewriter and paper."

"You have quite an argument," Simon admitted grimly.

Now he seemed to accept the fact that resistance was useless. With acceptance, he could show a renewal of his former ironical good humour.

"I think it would be a pity, though," Warlock said, "if you made both of us feel you'd had to be forced into this. How much better if we could co-operate freely! Think it over, and as you begin work I'm sure you'll feel more and more that I've done you a favour. The antagonisms will disappear as your enthusiasm for the project grows. I promise you."

As he spoke, he attempted to put his arm around Simon's shoulder and escort him to the door like an experienced businessman reassuring a nervous young subordinate. Since Warlock's proximity gave him the creeps, Simon managed to elude the embrace and face Warlock between the long table and the oak door.

"Incidentally," he said, "as long as we're going to be brothers in burglary, what's your real name?"

The other man looked at him strangely.

"Warlock," he said, as if answering the obvious.

"I mean the name your mother gave you," Simon said.

"A man's identity is a precious thing," Warlock said. "Don't tamper with it."

"No tampering intended," the Saint said quickly. "Do you prefer Warlock or Mr Warlock?"

Warlock raised his hand and pointed a trembling finger. His voice rose to a shrill pitch.

"Mr Klein, I warn you! People must take me seriously! I insist that people take me seriously!"

"I do take you seriously," Simon assured him. "I take you so seriously that I'm going to start racking my brains to conjure up so much trouble for Hermetico that the board of directors will wish they'd used that mine for nothing more important than curing cheese."

Warlock had an astonishing facility for changing moods.

"I knew," he said benevolently, "that you would soon see it my way."

He was grinning broadly as he led Simon to the door.

"We'll be keeping in touch, I suppose," said the Saint.

"Of course. Whatever assistance you require—a computer, technical help, my knowledge as a scientist—you have only to ask. You can dial number one on your phone and get me, or you can speak to Galaxy. She'll always be nearby."

"That'll brighten the coffee breaks."

Warlock hesitated before opening the door. He was all expansive bonhomie again.

"Mr Klein," he said, "don't tell your . . . secretary about the torture. There's no reason to upset her."

"Of course not," Simon said solemnly. "You're very considerate."

"Personally," Warlock said confidentially, "I wouldn't hurt a fly. Not personally. But did Napoleon ever personally shoot an enemy? I've often wondered. But the important thing is that he knew how to use people who didn't mind shooting."

3

When the Saint returned to his room, ushered by a silent Simeon Monk, he immediately heard a knock on the door beyond which Amity Little had purportedly been sleeping when he had been taken downstairs for his conference in the planning room.

"Thanks a lot, Sim," he said to the well-tailored gorilla who stood in the corridor as if waiting for some new command to make its tortuous way through his brain. "Why don't you go out in the garden and practise throwing yourself on electrified barbed wire? You could come in very handy when we storm Hermetico."

The Saint then closed that door of his room, leaving the bulk staring with dim perception from beneath the great bony shelf of his forehead. The knocking on the second door continued.

"Coming!" he called cheerily. "I'm so popular I can't keep up."

He crossed the huge sunny room and turned the handle. From somewhere nearby came the harsh clanging of an alarm bell.

"Oh, you shouldn't have done that!" Galaxy Rose cried from the other side of the door. "You should have said 'come in' and let me do it with my thumb."

"Well, go ahead and do it."

The alarm ceased, there was a gentle ping, and the door opened. Beside Galaxy stood Amity Little. Her short hair was freshly done and her elegant figure was dazzlingly displayed in a blue-flowered summer dress. She was smiling as happily as if her life had never been disrupted and was purring along completely on schedule.

"Amos!" she said. "How are you?"

"Fine, now that I see how you are."

The two girls came into his room. Amity did a slow-motion twirl to take in the decor and at the same time show off her dress.

"Wow!" she exclaimed. "You really rate! What a gorgeous pad!"

Simon had to fight back a smile at Amity's skilled transformation into just the sort of light-headed butterfly who might have been with Amos Klein on the night of his kidnapping.

"That's the reward of brain and fame," he said. "You should have been a writer."

"And you should have been a diplomat," she responded sweetly.

"You're treating her all right, aren't you?" he asked Galaxy.

Galaxy was like some ideal robot, indistinguishable from a real human female, but lacking the human disadvantage of jealousy.

"I'm doing my best," she said, beaming at Amity like an old school chum.

"I've had the most super bath," Amity chirped. "Soap jets all around! Coloured water with perfume and bubbles! And look at this dress."

"I've already looked," Simon said. "Come on in, Galaxy, and close the door. Let's make it a party."

"Thank you, master."

"Amos Klein!" Amity exclaimed. "Do you make her call you that?"

"I don't make her, I allow her, and unlike some women she appreciates a privilege when she has one." Simon caught Amity's eyes during his next words. "And what does she call you?"

"She calls me Amity Little, nuthead, because that's my name. They saw it on my driver's licence before I woke up. Where have you been and what have you been doing—or having done to you?"

"I've just returned from my investiture as commander-in-chief of SWORD. It's coronation day. Isn't somebody going to break a bottle of champagne over me?"

"I'll coronate you with a floor lamp," Amity said. "What are you babbling about?"

"Didn't Galaxy tell you anything?"

Galaxy shook her head.

"I'm not allowed to tell things," she said dutifully. "Only that you were all right and wouldn't be hurt. You mentioned champagne? Would you like some? It's in the cooler right here."

"Perfect," Simon said. "Bollinger, please, for three, and then would you order up some pheasant for lunch? On second thought, caviar first, and then pheasant."

Galaxy seemed happiest when taking orders.

"Right, master! Did you say for three?"

"Of course. You may be only a slave, but in these democratic days you're allowed to eat with the master."

Galaxy hurried to a cabinet which concealed a small refrigerator while Amity folded her arms and stared at Simon.

"Well, really, Amos, what's got into you?"

"Fifty thousand pounds for starters, and the grand panjandrumship of SWORD, not to mention the challenge of a bold adventure unequalled in modern times."

"You've either gone off your rocker or been reading your own movie reviews," said Amity. "While your concubines are preparing your feast, try to settle down and tell me what in the world is going on!"

Simon told her in terms which bordered on the enthusiastic, and as his narrative developed she managed to betray nothing except awed amazement.

"And this fellow who calls himself Warlock has actually created SWORD, gadgets and all?" she asked unbelievingly.

"So he tells me, and so far I have no reason to doubt his word. Apparently he's some sort of electronic genius, and I think we'll be amazed when we find out just how far he has gone." Simon paused to glance around the room. "I assume he can hear me, by the way, because if he has duplicated SWORD this room will have more bugs than a Bowery hop-house."

"And pictures," Amity added. "There'll be a man somewhere monitoring every move you make by closed-circuit television."

"More like monitoring every move Galaxy makes," Simon said.

He sat down in an armchair and settled his legs comfortably on a marble-topped table as Galaxy performed one of her undulatory transits, bringing Bollinger, caviar, and newly polished glasses. Simon opened the champagne and poured.

"To success," he said.

"Cheers," Amity said drily, as Galaxy echoed the Saint's words.

When they had drunk, Simon lifted his glass and scanned the upper walls and ceiling.

"And here's to all our friends out there in television land. Prepare to have your tapes censored, boys. I always throw an intimate little orgy to celebrate the beginning of a new book."

Galaxy giggled and tilted up her glass. She was on a leather ottoman near Simon's feet. Amity, who was in a neighbouring chair, showed subtle but perceptible signs of a less cheerful and co-operative disposition. She wrinkled her nose and rolled her eyes in the typical way of women who feel that their duty in life is to be ballast for the incorrigible silliness of men.

"And this book," she said. "It's to be the plan for cracking this big underground vault?"

"Exactly."

There was a rapping at the hall door.

"Come in," Simon called, "but don't forget to use your thumb."

Bishop, the bruised mock policeman, and Nero Jones, the semi-albino with the pale eyes of death, came in carrying the Hermetico model between them.

"Perfect timing, boys. Just put it over there by the window. Amity, I'd like you to meet two of my assistants, Mr Bishop and Mr—"

"Nero Jones," Amity said, completely awed. "It's fantastic! I'd recognize both of you anywhere, just from reading the books."

"Warlock's going to love you," Simon said.

"Miss Little," Bishop said politely.

Nero Jones merely inclined his head, then both men made several more trips to the hall, from which they brought an electric typewriter, a small tape recorder, several reams of paper, and a large assortment of such minor items as pencils, rubbers, and paper clips.

"Warlock says if there's anything else you need, just let us know."

"I won't hesitate."

Nero Jones handed Simon a sizeable book bound in black leather.

"The Hermetico dossier," he said. "And you left your money downstairs."

In his other hand he was carrying the attaché case with which Simon had been presented in the planning room. Jones set it on the floor.

"Thanks very much," the Saint said. "I don't have much to spend it on at the moment, but I might as well keep it around to cheer me up when the going gets tough."

Jones gave him a sour look and followed Bishop into the corridor. When they were gone, and the door was closed, Simon swung his feet to the floor, sat forward in his chair, and looked thoughtfully at the typewriter on its desk near the window.

"So," he said, "what it amounts to is this: either I come up with a scheme to knock over Hermetico, or little Amity gets herself taken slowly apart in SWORD's torture chamber."

Amity, who had gone to inspect the Hermetico model, suddenly spun around and stared.

"Who?" she squealed. "Me?"

"Yes, darling. If I don't perform, you'll have the honour of being the first person to try out some of those devilish machines in the basement."

Amity swallowed and pointed feebly at the floor.

"You mean . . . they really are . . . down there?"

"I haven't seen them, but I'm willing to take Warlock's word. I'll bet you another bottle of Bollinger that they're all down there, just as they were described with such grim and loving precision in the Charles Lake books." Simon sprawled back in his chair and regarded Amity's face with mildly sadistic satisfaction. "Don't you wish I didn't have such an active imagination?" he asked. "Or at least, not such a perverted, fiendish one?"

Amity clenched her fists and looked at the ceiling for some sign of a divine power which would keep her from murdering the Saint.

"Well, what are we going to do?" she finally asked. "I mean, I can't help it if there are twenty dozen people listening and watching: I'd like to know what we're going to do."

Simon got almost lazily to his feet and strolled to the window.

LESLIE CHARTERIS

"As the one who got us into this with his writing, I suppose it is up to me to get us out," he said. "All I can offer at the moment is what I said before. We'll make this Hermetico deal a big success, everybody'll be happy and rich, and nobody will get tortured."

Amity gawked at him, put her hands to her pretty head as if making certain it was still there, and turned around to appeal to the wall.

"But this is insane!"

"I wouldn't use that word around here too freely," Simon told her. "Let's refer to it as—visionary."

"More champagne?" Galaxy interrupted.

She had remained on the ottoman hugging her knees as she followed the conversation. Evidently she had occasionally refilled her glass from the bottle, too. The bottle was empty, and Galaxy showed definite symptoms of non-emptiness.

"No more for you," Simon said. "Master seems to have someone else to convince. Get him another bottle to lubricate his style and then run along and see how lunch is coming. I might be needing you later, and I don't want you paralysed."

She gave him an unsteady but dazzling smile, set another bottle of Bollinger from the refrigerator on the table, and waved at him from the hall door.

"Good luck," she cooed. "Just call me when you want a change."

"Thanks. And thanks for everything else, too. You've made my first day here absolute paradise."

When he and Amity were alone, she stood uncomfortably by the Hermetico model and looked at him with eyes that seemed bright with suppressed fury.

"I'd like to know just how she accomplished that," she said.

"What?" Simon asked.

"Paradise."

"Just a figure of speech. There's no such place on earth—but there is such a place as Hades, right here, unless you and I get to work."

He went quickly over to the phonograph which he had seen nested behind one of the wall panels beside the refrigerator. It slid out into the room for convenient use. Behind another sliding panel was an assortment of records.

"There," said Simon. "Pick out the loudest, swingingest thing you can find."

Amity obeyed, casting him a doleful look as he opened the second bottle of champagne and filled two fresh glasses.

"I thought you were going to work," she said.

"This is the way I go to work. You know that. I get my best ideas when I'm dancing—sort of like the Africans leaping themselves into a frenzy before the battle."

Suddenly, as Amity lowered the phonograph needle onto the record, the room was overwhelmed with a deafening roar of drums, grunts, twangings, metallic thwonks, and other primitive sounds.

"African enough for you?" she asked grimly.

"More than enough."

He gave her champagne, and then he took her into his arms and they began to dance. Simon, while he was pleased with the tumultuous quality of the music for its value as voice-camouflaging noise, did not match its pace with his dancing. He moved rhythmically but slowly, holding Amity close to him, his lips near her ear.

"They can't hear us now," he whispered. "You're doing fine. That was a convincing display of jealousy you put on a minute ago. Nobody would ever guess we met for the first time last night."

"I'm glad you approve," she said acidly. "I must be a born actress." She tilted her head back so that her eyes could meet his. "Really, Simon, what are we going to do? Are you really planning to co-operate with this maniac?"

The conversation continued in undertones, Simon trying to move his lips as little as a ventriloquist.

"He's as mad as a hatter, of course. But that doesn't make him a joke. Far from it. We've got to take him as seriously as he takes himself. Don't argue. We may not be able to talk long. We'll try to get out of here tonight. What are some of the things you invented to keep prisoners from escaping from headquarters?"

"Do you think this idiot playing Warlock really built them?"

"Very probably. There's an electrified steel fence all around the grounds, right?"

"Yes," she said, "and guards with dogs. In fact, take a look right now."

Simon led her past the open window. Across the green sweep of the lawn walked a hefty man in boots and jacket, a shotgun under his arm, a pair of Dobermanns snuffing at his heels.

"Perfect to the last detail," Amity muttered. "This is the most eerie thing I've ever been through."

"Let's concentrate on getting through it. What else besides the dogs? As I remember, the outer doors and windows are shuttered by a photo-electric device when it gets dark."

"Yes. And anyhow, unless we can find the television eyes and black them out, they can see anything we start to do as soon as we start it."

"You'll think of something," Simon said confidently. "After all, you're the genius they were really after. You invented SWORD and this house. Now invent a way to get out."

"I did, almost. For a character named Ansel Adams."

"I forget what happened," said the Saint.

Amity dropped her hand gloomily onto his shoulder.

"He got electrocuted."

4

After lunch with Amity Little in his room, the Saint put a new record on the phonograph and turned the volume up full blast.

"Dance?" he asked Amity, offering her his open arms.

"Simon," she sighed, not moving from her chair, "it's not that I don't like dancing with you, or that I don't think you're the most gorgeous man I've ever seen—but we've been at it for an hour."

Simon took both her hands and lifted her gently to her feet.

"You'll find it very beneficial," he said. "Stimulates circulation of the blood, helps digestion of pheasant, and infuriates Warlock."

They were dancing again now, Amity sagging and Simon bearing most of the weight of both their bodies.

"Infuriating Warlock isn't my idea of the smartest thing in the world," she whispered. "But after all, I'm only the one he'll torture to death, so why should I complain?"

"Exactly," Simon said cheerfully. "I want him good and worried. He's already invested more in Amos Klein than it costs to buy a winning football team. He could finish you off and it wouldn't make much difference, but if I just sat through your gruesome demise without cracking, he'd be in a real pickle. He'll do just about anything to appease me."

"You forget one minor point," Amity said. "I'm Amos Klein. If it comes to my gruesome demise, you can be sure Warlock's going to hear about that, too!"

"That won't be necessary," Simon assured her. "And he probably wouldn't believe you anyway. My idea at the moment is just to get him all upset so he'll come storming in here in a perfect mood for the line I want to toss him."

"How long do you expect that to take?" Amity asked with heartfelt weariness.

"Oh, Warlock has a low boiling point. Another hour or two, maybe."

Amity groaned softly and rested her forehead against Simon's bronzed lean cheek. He breathed the sweet scent of her hair and swayed with her slowly around the big, richly furnished room. There was a timelessness about the place, and it was not just the timelessness of imprisonment. It was almost as if the man who called himself Warlock had through the very power of his longing, actually succeeded in creating a world in which reality was frozen into the eternity of fiction—a world in a shimmering bubble exempt from the laws of time, the dreamy world of a boy reading away a summer's afternoon.

The only change was the imperceptible shifting of sunlight on the green lawn, and the gradual lengthening of the shadows of oaks and pines. The intervals between the slow recurrent passing of the watchman with his gun and dogs, like a precise and silent constellation, might have been minutes and might have been years.

"Amos," Amity whispered, "in *Earthquake Four* Charles Lake escaped from a castle."

"How?"

"By balloon. He jumped off the tower and floated right away."

"Where did he get the balloon?" Simon asked without any great enthusiasm.

"It was rolled up inside his umbrella. He filled it with gas from his cigarette lighter."

"Filled it with gas from his cigarette lighter," Simon repeated, non-committally.

"Yes. It was a special kind of gas."

"Otherwise known as hot air from the author."

Amity accepted the comment with a sigh and snuggled closer to the Saint.

"Who cares about escaping anyway?" she said. "It's nice here."

"Remember the converted plastic press in SWORD's basement?" he murmured in her ear. "Turns a human being into something like a burnt waffle."

Amity straightened up and looked at him disgustedly in the face.

"Oh, Simon, did you have to remind me of that?" she snapped.

"The name is Amos," he said quietly.

"Oh!" With a horrified look, Amity buried her face between his shoulder and neck. "Do you think they heard?"

"No. The music was loud. But . . ."

The Saint's words were broken off by the sudden opening of the hall door and the violent entrance into the room of a lividly agitated Warlock. The propensity of the subsurface of his large face to coagulate into blotches of purple and white was in full sway, making him seem at the point of fracturing into small varicoloured pieces like a dropped jigsaw puzzle. His wattles quivered as he stalked heavily across the room and snatched the tone arm from the phonograph record.

"I demand an explanation!" he stormed.

As the Saint stood unflinchingly, Amity clinging aghast to his arm, Warlock lifted the record and went through the dramatic gesture of smashing it against the corner of the phonograph. Unfortunately for Warlock's dignity, the record was made of unbreakable plastic and merely bounced unharmed from the impact. At last, after considerable strain, he managed to bend the disc with both hands until it broke. He flung the halves to the floor.

"I think you owe us an explanation," the Saint said coolly. "Are we to take it you aren't a music lover?"

Warlock pointed a trembling finger at him.

"You should take me seriously, Mr Klein! You've been dancing! Why?"

Simon shrugged.

"I like dancing."

Warlock clenched his teeth and clasped his fingers as if trying to hold himself together. He paced towards the window and took a deep breath. Glancing towards the open door, Simon saw that it was guarded by Monk and Nero Jones. When Warlock spoke again, it was in an unsteady but more subdued voice.

"Mr Klein, do you remember what SWORD did to the police sergeant in *Sunburst Five?*"

Amity clapped a hand to her mouth and burst out with a horrified, "Oh, no!"

Warlock, pleased to discover such a responsive member in his audience, turned to speak directly to her.

"The equipment is fully operational in the cellar. The tubes can be filled with acid in one minute."

"You wouldn't!" Amity gasped.

"Oh, but I would," replied Warlock. His voice had become almost a purr. He addressed Simon. "Your lovely young friend may live to regret your devilish imagination."

Simon shook his head with mournful calm, regarding his chubby antagonist as a patient teacher might regard a disappointing pupil.

"Warlock, I'm ashamed of you," he said quietly.

Warlock was startled.

"Ashamed?" he said.

The Saint's lugubrious expression would have wilted a whole vase of freshly cut flowers.

"You're out of character," he lamented. "In my books you were evil, of course, but you were also intelligent and sensitive."

"So?" Warlock asked.

"So now you're acting like a mentally deficient water buffalo."

The purple splotches which disfigured Warlock's face diffused into a uniform scarlet coating. His mouth opened and produced a questioning exhalation.

"Have you any idea," Simon continued, "how difficult it is to be a writer? Surely a man of your aesthetic sensibilities must realize that it's not a simple matter of ordering up a lot of pre-cut ideas and hammering them together like a man building a dog-house."

Warlock watched, somewhat abashed, as Simon turned towards the window with a martyred sigh, closed his eyes, and pressed the thumb and forefinger of his left hand on either side of his nose just below the bridge.

"It's a constant struggle," he went on. "Or maybe struggle isn't the best word, since inspiration is something that can't be forced. It's like . . . fishing. You settle yourself down, you drop in your hook, and you hope." Simon confronted Warlock directly again. "Do you really think it's as easy as saying after Monday comes Tuesday?"

Warlock contorted his little mouth in embarrassment.

"Well, I . . . I don't think I have ever underestimated your genius," he said hesitantly.

"Yet you expect me to work while I'm a prisoner?" The Saint changed his stance so that only Amity could see his face as he gave her an encouraging wink. "It's like . . . expecting a plant to blossom without sunlight or water."

Amity joined in.

"It's like . . . locking up your goose without food or water and expecting it to lay golden eggs."

Simon flinched only slightly at the simile as Warlock turned up his palms in flustered appeal.

"You have all the food you need," he said helplessly. "You have everything a man could want."

"Except freedom," said Simon quickly.

Amity was shaking her head at Warlock.

"You really don't understand the artist's soul, do you?" she said. "Do you think you can stifle him . . . cage him up like an animal?"

"And expect me to create?" Simon joined in.

"Ridiculous!" snorted Amity.

Warlock made mute gestures which clearly were a plea for silence.

"Mr Klein, you make me ashamed," he said, when he was finally given a chance. "I had no intention, I assure you, of stifling you. On the other hand, under the circumstances, I couldn't possibly allow you to leave these grounds at this point. And please don't think I'm so naive as to believe you need the run of the entire British Isles before your inspiration can blossom."

Warlock made an expressive motion of his plump hand which symbolized the flowering of Amos Klein's orchid-like imagination.

"How about the grounds, then," Amity suggested. "You could let us out of the house, at least. I'm sure that would help, wouldn't it, Amos?"

"I suppose," said the Saint, who was sulking near the wall.

"It's better than nothing," Amity insisted. "May we go out in the garden then?"

Warlock nodded reluctantly.

"Very well. Mr Klein may go out. Galaxy will go along to keep you company."

"What about me?" Amity asked.

"I'm sorry, Miss Little," Warlock replied, looking more sly than sorry. "I can't have you both out of the house at once. Just a simple precaution. And anyway, it's not the health of your imagination that we're concerned about, is it?"

Warlock smiled as Amity flung herself down furiously in a chair and glared at the rug. Simon patted her on the shoulder as he went by on his way to the open door.

"Don't feel bad," he said. "Creativity deserves a few privileges, after all."

Ten minutes later the Saint was strolling across the lawn which until then he had seen only from the window of his room. Beside him strolled Galaxy Rose, instructed by Warlock to keep silent so as not to disturb Amos Klein's priceless meditations. She dutifully kept the slow pace, staying a half-step behind, glancing frequently at the Saint's face as if she expected it to glow a brilliant green when some striking idea popped into his head.

As for Simon, his thoughts were at least as active as Galaxy was capable of imagining, but directed towards an entirely different object than cracking into Hermetico. The Saint's particular interest at the moment was not breaking into anything, but breaking out of Warlock's private fortress.

"Is that the only fence?" he asked.

He had stopped at the edge of the expanse of grass which sloped down from one side of the large stone house. Beyond the lawn was a hedge of rose bushes, and beyond them a border of evergreens which fringed the property all round. Through the needles of the trees Simon could see the tall chain link steel fence topped with barbed wire. Beyond the steel fence, preventing it being seen from outside the property, was an antique and respectable stone wall of the sort that men used to surround their private patch of the planet with before such selfish impulses became an offence to the state and an invitation to annihilation by tax collectors—who unlike less subtle thieves are hindered neither by walls nor locks and doors.

"If you think I'm going to say anything that might help you get out of here, you're wrong," Galaxy said loudly.

The Saint glanced around him at the white and yellow roses, the trees, and the grass.

"So they've got microphones even out here," he mused.

Galaxy snapped her eyes at him almost angrily.

"It wouldn't matter whether they did or not," she said. "I wouldn't help you escape because I'm as anxious as everybody else for this to work out all right."

His hands in his pockets, the Saint continued his leisurely circuit of the lawn.

"That's right," he said. "Warlock promised you half a million for this Hermetico caper, didn't he?"

Galaxy stared at him with surprise and suspicion.

"How did you know?"

"You forget," Simon replied. "I wrote the books. Warlock may be a brilliant organizer, but he's no original thinker. Everything he's done up to now has been based on what he's read."

"You're not telling me anything."

"Okay, tough girl, but don't say I didn't warn you."

"About what?" she asked.

"About what happens in the new book."

"The one you're supposedly writing?"

"Yes."

Galaxy compressed her lips as if trying to control her voice.

"Well," she said irritably, "what happens?"

"You never get the half-million. Warlock double-crosses you."

Galaxy looked lost for a moment, then exasperated.

"Don't waste your breath," she said. "I've seen that movie twenty times."

"Which movie is that?" Simon asked guilelessly.

"The one where the hero turns the bad characters against one another by making them think they're planning to double-cross one another. I'm not that dumb."

"At least you're smart enough to see who the hero is," Simon rejoined.

He and the girl continued their walk. His probings had convinced him that however eager she was to please him, she had no discernible intention of risking her neck or her promised half-million pounds by overstepping the limits which Warlock had imposed.

"Why can't you be happy?" she asked in a softer and more persuasive voice than she had used for the past several minutes. "Why fight it? Write a happy ending for everybody."

"Maybe you're right," Simon said, but he was not particularly listening.

His eye had just picked out the window of his room, whose location he had carefully pinpointed before he left it. There was nothing remarkable about it. It was just like all the other windows in the front of the house. But there was a much more humble feature of architecture near it which the Saint found completely fascinating: a fat black drainpipe running vertically from beneath the eaves above his window to the ground thirty feet below. That venerable relic of twentieth-century plumbing's adolescence would ordinarily have been of no interest whatsoever to anybody, but to the Saint it was the closest thing he had yet seen to a flaw in Warlock's comfortable prison.

He pretended to have noticed nothing, and turned his attention to the front drive, which led from a double garage beside the house to a locked wire gate inside the older wooden one of the stone wall. One side of the garage was open, and outside it Frug was washing an immense black limousine of the kind sported by embassies and departments of foreign affairs. Frug self-consciously attended to his work and avoided watching the Saint and Galaxy.

"Is the gate electrified too?" Simon asked his companion.

"If you know so much, you must know that," she said archly.

"It's electrified," said the Saint. He nodded towards the limousine. "And that hearse over there—it's from *Hurricane Eight*, I assume."

"Right. It's got everything just the way you described it."

"Amazing. I'd like a ride in it."

Galaxy smiled.

"I'm sure you would—but you'd have a lot better chance of taking one if you'd get down to work instead of worrying about escaping."

Simon shook his head and sighed as he turned towards the front entrance of the house.

"That's a woman for you—always brimming with practical suggestions. Work brings freedom, does it? I'm afraid I've got to admit it: Warlock has me stymied. I can't do much but play along and hope it all works out for the best."

Galaxy hugged his arm and snuggled close to him.

"You'll be glad," she assured him. "It is best this way."

Simon's secret thoughts found expression only in another brief glance at the black drainpipe which ran from roof to ground. Then, behind the glass of one of the ground floor windows, he glimpsed the face of Warlock peering out at him, like a warning personified.

"You can be sure," he murmured, "I'll try to make everything work out for the best."

"For me too?" Galaxy insisted.

"For you especially," Simon said, as earnestly as he could.

CHAPTER FOUR:

HOW AMITY CAME TO BED AND

NERO JONES LOST A SHOE

1

An observer looking in on the Saint's bedroom that night—as one was—would have thought he had nothing in mind but sleep. He came out of his bathroom magnificently arrayed in one of the dozen pairs of pyjamas contributed by Warlock to his wardrobe—a composite of sunsets, peacocks' tails, and fireworks displays which only a man of icy nerves and considerable humour could have worn without flinching—and made a circuit of the room turning out all the lights. When only the single reading lamp on the bed's headboard was left, he stretched, yawned, and gave the room a last glance.

There was a half-filled sheet of paper in the typewriter, and a table nearby was littered with more sheets of paper covered with scrawl and figures the sight of which must have gladdened Warlock's heart if he had looked in on them via television before his retirement. It was just as well, for the sake of his gladdened heart, that he did not look at the papers more closely, since the figures were meaningless and the scrawl was largely illegible.

Except for the papers and some minor disarrangements of the furniture which further attested to Amos Klein's and Amity Little's labours on the Hermetico project, the room was as it had been in the morning . . . with two important exceptions. At nine that evening, as sunset had faded from the sky, a steel shutter, its movement preceded by an alarm bell reminiscent of those sounded on ships during the testing of watertight doors, had slid down over Simon's window and clanked firmly into place with the authoritative sound of something that had come to stay until it was ready to leave. At the same time, as the Saint knew without seeing, windows all over the building were undergoing the same sealing process, as were the outer doors.

The presence of the tight steel shutter over the bedroom window was one of the two changes which had taken place since morning. The second was the fact that the door between Simon's and Amity Little's room was open. That was the result of no oversight on SWORD's part, but of a convincing and passionate argument on Simon's. He could not work, he insisted, without the presence of his friend and secretary, and he often did his best work in the middle of the night. While other men slept away their drab little lives, his brain would suddenly explode in a sparkling shower of ideas which cried out for immediate transplantation to paper. Without Amity on constant call he could not guarantee that such nocturnal eruptions would not dissipate into outer darkness, lost forever—and with them Warlock's dreams of wealth and power.

Warlock, convinced by house telephone, had seen the logic of the argument and could think of no special danger in granting Simon's request. Since there was no chance of escape anyway, what could be the harm in allowing the eccentric artist whatever companion he desired?

So Amity, her room already darkened, waited until Simon's would be the same.

He gave a last yawn for the benefit of the television monitor, then drew the heavy curtains all around his bed and climbed into the tent like shelter. Although the reading lamp inside the canopy was still on, he knew that from the point of view of the television eye the room was in total darkness. He had satisfied himself already that there was no lens in his bed, but there was a microphone in what appeared to be a coin-sized decorative grille in the base of the reading lamp.

In Simon's pyjama shirt pocket were several Band-Aids he had taken from the medicine cabinet in the bathroom—which was thoughtfully equipped with everything from cologne to milk of magnesia. He tore the backing off one of them, coughing as he did so. He had already prepared a thick pad of facial tissue, also supplied in the bathroom. Coughing several more times, he then let his breathing become deep and regular. Then, very slowly, he placed the pad of tissue over the microphone aperture and taped it into place with the Band-Aid. A second piece of adhesive completed the seal, and that particular microphone was deaf.

Next, the Saint turned out the reading lamp, putting the room in total darkness, and left his bed. Wary of other microphones still active, he crept across the rug to his desk and felt for the small tape recorder he had left in one corner. All he had to do then was to cough to cover the sound of depressing the playback switch. The tape began to move. He could feel the turning of the spool. Then he heard the sound of his own breathing coming from the loudspeaker. A moment later he heard a cough and a restless rustling of cloth. It was a production he had carried out carefully during the afternoon while he and Amity had worked on the Hermetico project. The tape contained nothing for forty-five minutes except sounds of breathing and occasional coughing. By the time it fell silent the Saint and Amity—hopefully—would be miles away.

Simon went back to his canopied bed and waited in absolute blackness until he heard a movement of the curtains and Amity crawled in beside him.

"It's me," she whispered directly into his ear.

"Surprise. Now let's see if I can guess who 'me' is."

"Rat. Just concentrate on getting us out of this padded cell."

Simon made certain the curtains were drawn tightly. He turned on the reading light. Amity, fully dressed in mini-skirt, sweater, and low-heeled shoes, sat up self-consciously.

"Literature makes strange bedfellows," he remarked. "Do you have the fingernail scissors?"

"Yes."

Simon stood up on the mattress with the small pair of sharply pointed scissors in one hand. With the other hand he grasped the velvet roof of the canopy.

"Now turn out the light," he whispered.

The following stage of the operation was carried out in silence. Simon worked the scissors through the cloth above him and slowly cut out a circle of the material roughly two feet in diameter. He handed the piece of cloth down to Amity, who held his legs to steady him during the next part of his work.

He had already ascertained during the afternoon that the ceiling was not the original, which probably had been plaster long cracked with age, but was modern plasterboard in two by two foot squares nailed directly to the beams.

"Are you sure," he had said to Amity in the afternoon during one of their later dances, "that SWORD doesn't have some sort of an alarm system rigged to the ceilings?"

"I'm not sure of anything," she had answered rather emotionally. "Do you think I can read Warlock's mind? Do you think I built the place or something?"

"In any of your books, was the ceiling rigged?" he had asked firmly.

"No, I never thought of that."

"Not very bright."

"Oh, shut up."

"Be grateful," Simon had told her soothingly. "That little oversight may save our lives."

Now, however, as he actually brought the point of the scissors into contact with one of the cracks between sections of plasterboard, he felt more hope than confidence. Could he be certain that Warlock would have followed Amos Klein's works slavishly enough to include even the oversights in the construction of his headquarters? There was no guarantee that the first penetration of the scissors, or the first prying away of a section of plasterboard, would not result in a deafening and potentially deadly eruption of alarms and pounding feet in hallways all over the building.

Simon slipped the point of the scissors between the adjoining pieces of ceiling material until he felt the scissors press against the wooden beams to which the plasterboard was nailed. There was no alarm. Not breathing, but hearing the sound of his own breathing from the tape recorder, Simon cautiously moved the scissors to one side, using them as a lever to pry the board from the wooden beam. Instinctively he worked slowly, as if he thought he could slam the board back into place at the first sound of ringing bells and thereby avoid detection, even though he knew that one split second of alarm would guarantee catastrophe at this point.

Still, he worked slowly, and not only through an unreasoning desire to avoid an alarm which, if it existed, could not be avoided, but because of the necessity for silence. Three nails held the square of plasterboard to a beam on each of its sides, which meant that the Saint, with his tiny pair of scissors, had to work loose six nails without a squeak of metal in wood nor a rattle of the already loosened edges of the board against the beams. Envying the recorded ease with which his lungs had enjoyed their oxygen that afternoon, he breathed with silent caution and eased the nails from their seats in the wood.

The next to the last was stubborn. It had no intention of budging without a fight, and when it did it creaked from the hard wood with what sounded to Simon's ears like the legendary shriek of a mandrake torn living from the earth.

"Shh!" said Amity.

Simon restricted his reaction to vivid mental images of Amity hanging by her thumbs from the ceiling of Warlock's subterranean torture chamber. Silently he passed down the square of plasterboard, and his companion slipped it under the bed.

"Now," he whispered, "up you go."

He formed a stirrup with his hands in order to boost her through the hole in the ceiling. She steadied one of her feet there.

"Ready," she whispered.

"Down!" Simon snapped.

"What?"

"Someone's coming."

Simon dropped Amity onto the bed without much regard for how she landed. The footsteps he had heard approaching in the corridor were at the door. There were four rapid knocks.

"Keep still," Simon whispered to Amity. "Get your clothes off, and if anybody pokes his head in here try to keep his eyes on you and hope he doesn't notice the hole in the ceiling."

Amity's protesting gasps were cut short as he rolled quickly from the bed, drawing the curtains behind him. Almost blind in the darkness, he managed to locate the tape recorder and slap down the "off" button just as a gentle ping announced the unlocking of his room's door. As it opened, he staggered bleary-eyed into the fan of bright light that came in from the hall.

"What is it?" he mumbled. "What's happening?"

The ample form of Bishop presented itself on the threshold.

"I heard something squeak," he said, half belligerently and half apologetically.

"And you woke me up to tell me that?" Simon cried, working himself rapidly into a temperamental rage. "Why didn't you call your mother?"

Bishop would have stepped into the room if Simon had not blocked his way.

"I'm supposed to investigate anything strange," he muttered.

He was doing his best to investigate, going on tiptoe from one foot to the other as he bobbed from side to side trying to see around the Saint's shoulders.

"Well I'm here," Simon shouted at him. "What more do you want? If you'd prefer total silence you'd better send me home or shut down your blasted listening post!"

There was a sound of running feet behind Bishop, and Warlock himself hove into view, puffing mightily. He was clutching a quilted red robe around him, and he had either lost or not taken time to put on one of his loose-fitting slippers.

"What's wrong?" he called.

"I . . ." Bishop began, but Simon interrupted.

"Wrong?" he yelled. "I'll tell you what's wrong! These idiots of yours are harassing me to death." He pointed at Bishop, almost prodding his nose. "Do you know what's wrong with this one? He heard something squeak! Can you believe that?" Simon's voice rose to a tremulous climax as he invoked Warlock's incredulity. "Can you believe it? He heard something squeak!"

"What is this, Bishop?" Warlock asked. "I told you to call me only in an emergency."

"I . . ." Bishop began. Then he paused, red-faced. "I heard this sort of loud squeak, and I reckoned . . ."

"He reckoned any excuse was enough to let him barge in here and wake me up in the middle of the night!" said the Saint. "And I absolutely cannot function without eight hours of uninterrupted sleep! I cannot!" He thumped his fist against his open palm. "I absolutely cannot."

"Well, I'm sorry, Mr Klein," said Bishop, "but I distinctly heard . . ."

"A squeak," Simon said.

"Is that all, Bishop?" Warlock asked sternly.

"It was a loud squeak," Bishop said. He tried to see around the Saint into the room. "Maybe I'd better check the bed," he said defensively.

"Oh, wonderful!" said Simon, carried to new heights of sarcasm by the obvious cretinism of Warlock's staff. "Check the bed! Magnificent." He flung out an inviting arm. "Please do. Please. I don't know which of us will be most embarrassed, but if it'll earn me a few hours' rest, you're more than welcome."

"Bishop," said Warlock, "go back to the monitoring room. I'll speak to you later. In the meantime, do not disturb me or Mr Klein unless you're quite certain something is wrong."

"Yes," Simon called after Bishop. "Squeak or no squeak. As long as I'm cooped up here I'll squeak all I please. I'll stay up all night storming around the room shouting 'SQUEAK SQUEAK SQUEAK!' at the top of my lungs if I feel like it!"

"I'm sorry, Mr Klein," Warlock said. "People are a bit jumpy and over-eager, but I'll try to prevent you from being bothered."

"Thank you," Simon said, and closed the door in his face.

This time he did not bother to restart the tape recorder. Instead he went straight to the bed and climbed between the curtains.

"Oh!" Amity choked.

"I can't see a thing," Simon assured her. "Get dressed again and let's go."

"I never got all the way," she whispered.

He could hear her tugging something on as he stood up and relocated the hole in the ceiling.

"Well, that bit of modesty could have cost your life," Simon told her. "It doesn't matter now, though. Just hurry up."

"For heaven's sake, I'm doing my best!"

A moment later he had hoisted her through the bed's canopy and the hole in the ceiling. Proceeding entirely by touch, he stretched his arms above his head and found one of the beams exposed by the removal of the plasterboard. He could reach just high enough to grasp the top of the beam with his fingers. Using the bed as a springboard, he pushed off with the tips of his toes and lifted himself up in one smooth motion so that his head and shoulders were above the beam. With a renewed swing of his body and perfectly co-ordinated pressure of his arm muscles, he brought his hips and legs up through the hole and came to rest seated on the beam.

"Are you all right?" Amity whispered. "I can't see a thing."

"I'm here," Simon assured her. "Be sure you stay on the beams. You'll drop right down through the ceiling otherwise."

"It seems to have a kind of floor over this way," she told him. "And I feel some wires I think."

"Don't touch anything. That drainpipe I saw this afternoon should be right opposite us. This way."

"Can we have a light now?"

"Wait until we get over where the roof meets the floor."

Simon worked his way gingerly from beam to beam, moving towards the front of the house. He could hear Amity coming along behind him.

"Can you feel the roof yet?" she whispered.

"Not yet."

He had been reaching above his head frequently without making contact with anything but empty air. Almost immediately after Amity asked her question his fingers touched a slanting rafter. Between it and its neighbour, which the Saint quickly located, was a band of felt insulation. Above the insulation, he knew, were the tiles of the roof.

"Here we are," he said. "Come up alongside, but don't stand up straight or you'll smash your head."

"Shall I use my lighter now?"

"Yes, but try to keep the light from getting down into the bedroom."

A second later Amity flicked her lighter and produced a tiny flame. Small as it was, in comparison with the total darkness of a moment before it seemed as bright as a miniature sun. The attic was compartmented. Undoubtedly some of the other areas contained their share of the building's elaborate equipment. The section in which Simon and Amity found themselves was small and empty except for wiring.

"Now I'll strip off some of this insulating material and you take the tiles when I hand them to you."

He used the scissors to help tear away the felt. In the wavering flame he could see the overlapping tiles which formed the roof itself. He had to be careful not to send any of the tiles skittering down the roof to the ground. Luckily the pitch of the roof was shallow, a fact he had taken into account while evolving his plan in the afternoon. It was fairly simple to free one of the tiles and carefully push it out of place.

"Put the light out now," he instructed Amity. "We don't want some guard spotting that from out in the garden."

She obeyed, and Simon—since the first tile he had loosened would not fit through the hole its removal had created—reached up through the hole and laid the tile on the gentle slope of the roof. The second tile which he pulled free came easily through the hole. He brought it down and handed it to Amity, who set it aside on one of the beams which formed the floor of the attic.

In a matter of seconds, Simon had pulled loose and passed down several tiles and made a hole in the roof large enough for him and Amity to climb through.

"Oh, isn't it beautiful?" she said in a hushed voice. "Sky, fresh air, stars . . . and freedom."

She was kneeling beside Simon, looking up through the hole, in a kind of prayerful rapture.

"It is beautiful," he said, "but I'm afraid this was only the easy part, for us. We'll have to save our celebrating for the other side of that electrified fence."

He climbed easily up onto the roof, sat next to the hole he had made in the tiles, and reached down to take Amity's hands in order to help her follow him.

"Easy now," he soothed her. "There's nothing to it. Don't flail around."

Unfortunately, she did flail around. Instead of arriving beside the Saint in one simple movement, which was all that would have been necessary, she struggled like a cat trying to scale the side of a gravel heap. She ended up with her upper half on the roof and her legs kicking below. In her scrambling to go the rest of the way, she dislodged one of the tiles from the lower edge of the hole. With a loud clatter it rattled down the roof, bounced over the edge of the eaves, and a moment later clumped into the shrubbery below.

"Oh my," said Amity, who was now lying flat on the roof next to Simon.

A dog had set up a vicious barking in front of the house. As the Saint prostrated himself alongside Amity, he could hear the voice of a man, apparently speaking to the dog. The glare of an electric light playing over the lower part of the building reflected above the eaves. Then the dog was quiet, there was some rustling in the shrubs, and the footsteps of the guard finally moved away. There was no more detectable light except from the starry sky.

"He must have decided it wasn't anything," Simon whispered.

He raised himself to a sitting position again and stretched his neck in order to see down into the yard below.

"Let's hope," Amity said. "What now?"

Simon pointed towards the darkness beyond the eaves.

"Follow that falling tile," he said cheerily.

"I usually write in a helicopter at this point." Amity said.

"I'm afraid you stacked the deck in the bad guys' favour this time. The forces of sweetness and light are going to have to climb down the drainpipe. Just follow me. Hold on to the eaves, swing your legs down and catch the pipe, then climb down as fast as you can."

2

It was as uncomplicated as Simon predicted. The descent was accomplished with a minimum of noise, and even Amity managed to creep through the shrubbery without attracting the keen ears of the watchdogs. From the corner of the house she and Simon could see both the garage and the front gate. A guard without a canine companion stood by the gate. Simon's eyes followed the paved drive which led from the gate to the garage, where he had seen Frug washing the limousine that afternoon.

"You're sure that guard has no way to shut down the electricity in the fence or to unlock the gate?" he asked Amity.

"I'm sure—if Warlock followed my books," she answered. "Only Warlock can do that, from inside the house."

"Let's just hope he was as thorough when he designed that limousine. If I understand you, the auxiliary ignition switch is recessed under the steering column."

"Right. Warlock almost got captured once when he lost the keys to the car, so he had the second switch installed. Only he is supposed to know about it."

"Well, then, here goes. Flatten yourself against the garage door as soon as we get to it."

The distance between house and garage was only a few paces. The guard at the gate did not notice the shadowy figures darting from the shelter of one wall to another.

"Now, something I just thought of," Simon said. "Won't these garage doors be wired into the alarm system?"

"Yes, but there's a switch you can throw by pushing one of the bricks down here next to the ground." Amity knelt down and felt the lower bricks beside the articulated metal door. "Yes. Here. This one moved when I pressed it. It gives me the most uncanny feeling. He's thought of everything."

"Including the extra ignition switch, I hope! Now, the guard may hear the door going again, so get ready for some fast action. I'll see what I can do with this lock."

"Maybe it's not locked," suggested Amity.

"It must be."

But when Simon tried turning the handle his hand met no resistance. He and Amity each took one of the doors and swung them quietly outwards. In the deeper darkness of the garage's interior glinted the black limousine, its nose towards the door.

"Too easy," Simon whispered as they ran to either side of the big car. "Don't tell me Mr Warlock was good enough to leave the car open too."

The limousine's windows were up, but the doors were not locked.

"Don't look gift horses in the mouth," Amity said.

"Where's that ignition switch?"

Their hands groped beneath the steering wheel. Suddenly light flared through the front window of the car.

"It's the guard!" Amity cried, no longer bothering to hold her voice to a whisper. "He's coming this way!"

Simon's fingers found the small metal button beneath the steering column. The engine rumbled. Simon engaged the automatic shift and jammed the gas pedal to the floor. The wheels whined on the cement floor of the garage, propelling the giant limousine out along the drive like a shell from a cannon. The guard with the light was in the centre of the pavement. He dived for the grass. One of the patrol dogs came racing towards the car, barking wildly, its handler running behind it with a shotgun.

Those were Simon's last impressions in the seconds it took the car to cover the ground between the garage and the wire mesh gate. He had already reached a speed of fifty miles an hour. He would have liked more, but the gate seemed to expand directly ahead of him in the car lights. The shotgun roared at almost point blank range, and the full charge spat harmlessly against the window just six inches from Amity's cheek.

"Good glass," Simon had time to say. "Hang on."

The front of the car ripped into the wire fence, creating an explosion of sparks as the deadly electric current was shorted in a hundred places. Next came the crunching sound of splintering wood as the limousine hurtled through the second gate immediately beyond the first. It was free then, roaring out of the volcanic incandescence of its escape into a straight stretch of dark country road.

"Are we out?" Amity asked in a quavering voice.

She had thrown herself to the floor and covered her head with her hands.

"We're out," Simon said. "You can come up now."

He slowed the limousine to a reasonable speed as Amity sat beside him. She pointed to the spider web of cracks and pockmarks made by the shotgun blast.

"Look."

Her voice was weak.

"This thing is like a tank," Simon said, patting the door affectionately. "Congratulations on furnishing it with bullet-proof glass."

"Thanks, but I don't even want to think about those books again, much less write any." She turned to look out the back window. "There's nobody after us yet."

"I wonder where we are. Watch for road signs."

Amity turned and sat back in the seat with a deep sigh. She lowered her window halfway so that she could see beyond the cracked glass.

"We've made it," she said. "We've done the impossible, do you realize that? We've escaped from SWORD!"

Simon glanced into the dark rectangle of the rearview mirror.

"Maybe," he said.

"Maybe?" whimpered Amity.

"I'd feel a lot better if the impossible had been a little more difficult."

"Well, for heaven's sake don't worry about it! We're out now. What can they do about it?"

Almost simultaneously with her last word, several things happened at once. The window she had lowered shot up with the force of a guillotine. The car engine died completely without so much as a splutter. There was a rapid series of clicks as the door locks automatically popped into closed positions.

"I wish you hadn't asked that question," Simon said to Amity.

The car was rolling to a standstill on the unlighted road as its own lights were extinguished by whatever force had shut off the engine. Simon pumped the accelerator without result. Working the auxiliary ignition button which had originally started the car produced not even a click.

"What happened?" Amity gasped.

"You tell me," said Simon. "You wrote the script."

Amity, frowning, shook her head.

"There was never anything like this. Let's get out of here. It looks like a crossroads up ahead . . ."

"I'm afraid you'll find that impossible," Simon said. "My door is sealed shut."

"Oh, no! So is mine."

Suddenly a red light began to glow in the centre of the instrument panel and a voice issued from the radio grille.

"This is Warlock speaking. This recording of my voice was activated by the same device which automatically trapped you and cut off the electrical system of the car. Your location will be easily traced by a tracking device which picks up a continuous signal broadcast from the car you have so foolishly stolen. I suggest that you make yourself comfortable. There is no way to escape, and very shortly several persons will arrive to take you in custody."

"So Warlock isn't completely unoriginal," the Saint said when the recording fell silent.

"Oh, dear," Amity said sheepishly.

"Oh, dear, what?" Simon asked.

"In a short story I wrote—before the first book—there was something . . . like this."

"My compliments to your memory. What's the trick for getting out?"

"No trick. It wasn't important. It didn't happen to important characters."

"Well, we're important characters, and I've no intention of sitting around here like a chicken in a box waiting for the butcher. Get your head out of the way, please. Maybe that shotgun weakened the glass."

Simon swung his legs above the girl's lap, braced his hands behind him, and gave the damaged window a double-footed kick which would have taken most car doors completely off their hinges. The thick window was completely unchanged.

"As I said, good glass," he remarked ruefully. "I'll try the back way."

He climbed quickly over into the back seat and proceeded, in effect, to pull it apart.

"What are you doing?" Amity asked.

"Trying to get these cushions loose so we can get back into the boot."

"Isn't there anything between the seat and the boot?"

"Generally just some cloth, at least in places."

"I didn't know that," Amity said.

"Good. If you had you'd have figured a way to keep us from getting out."

Simon had pulled loose the back cushion, revealing a strip of black leatherette material. He ripped it aside. There was nothing else between him and the boot.

"Your lighter, please," he said.

Amity leaned over from the front seat to hand it to him.

"Don't blow us up."

"That might be the fastest way out."

He put his head and shoulders through the hole he had created and flicked on the lighter to illuminate the stark interior of the boot.

"Can you get through that little space?" Amity called after him.

"Yes. You follow. I'm going to pry open the lock with a screwdriver."

The Saint snaked his way into the boot, took a screwdriver from the kit he had discovered beside the spare tyre, and with the lighter beside him commenced his attack on the lock of the boot lid. He had trouble making out Amity's words.

"Simon . . ."

The Saint, having more important things to do than indulge in conversation, grunted and continued his work.

"Simon . . ."

He twisted his head so that he could speak over his shoulder.

"What is it?"

His answer came not from Amity Little but from the lock on which he had been working. Magically it moved, the boot lid swung upwards, and there, with pistols in their hands, stood Nero Jones and Simeon Monk.

"Come out, Mr Klein, wherever you are . . ."

The singsong, triumphantly jolly voice belonged to Warlock, whose unmistakable silhouette came into view behind his cohorts.

"Get out," said Nero Jones with less cordiality.

The Saint was no advocate of suicide disguised as daring. Had he been, his career would have ended not many weeks after it began. It is quite simple to get killed making rash attacks on armed criminals, and the Saint could see nothing heroic, much less very bright, in obviously foredoomed gestures. On the other hand, the precise calculation of risks was his speciality, and in this particular situation the odds favoured his survival in reasonably good health no matter what he did. As Amos Klein, he was simply too valuable to kill, or even to injure, so he could afford to take greater chances than if he had been up against a pair of trigger-happy gorillas with orders to shoot to kill.

"Give me a hand, would you?" he said resignedly. "I'm jammed in here."

He was flat on his stomach in the boot of the car. He held out his left hand as his right hand, hidden by his body, closed around the cold solidity of an iron jack handle. Jones and Monk glanced back towards Warlock, who nodded. Monk stepped forward to help, while his comrade increased his vigilance.

"Thanks, dear old ape," said the Saint, and as soon as Monk grasped his hand he yanked the huge man forward with all his strength.

Simeon Monk was only graceless but top-heavy. His great weight was off balance in the Saint's favour to begin with, and he sprawled like a crashing tree head-first into the boot. With the same sudden movement that toppled Monk, Simon jerked himself forward and rolled from the boot to his feet on the ground. The jack handle simultaneously became a short range weapon of deadly efficiency. Before Nero Jones could so much as stagger back in the first eye-blink of surprise, Simon had hurled the metal bar at his midsection with a force that made the air whistle. Then came Jones's explosive groan as he jack-knifed forward and stumbled writhing to the earth.

The whole manoeuvre had taken not much more time than the striking of a snake, even including the slamming of the boot lid down on the backs of Simeon Monk's thighs. Above his howl came Warlock's shrill voice.

"Stop, Mr Klein!"

Simon had planned to improvise his dealings with Warlock. The man, no fighter, and deprived by his own ambitions of the freedom to use a weapon, should have been no match. So it was with a certain appalled shock that the Saint spun around to face his enemy and found himself looking into the barrel of a steadily outstretched pistol which Warlock aimed at his chest and, with what seemed an interminable movement of his trigger finger, fired.

But there was no sound of exploding gunpowder, and the stinging sensation Simon felt in the muscle between chest and left shoulder was not the burning, bone-shattering impact of a lead slug. He looked in surprise and saw an inch-long shaft of shiny metal protruding from his pyjama shirt where the pistol's projectile had hit him. He groped for it, testing as he touched it for barbs that might tear his flesh if he tried to pull it out, and then numbing sleep seemed to shoot through his veins like a flood of icy ether deluging his whole body. The last thing he knew was impotent fury at this second triumph of Warlock's drugs over his own body and will.

3

"Mr Klein," Warlock said quietly, "I see no reason to lecture you or waste time on elaborate threats. We understood one another before you attempted to escape. Everything will go forward just as we planned then, except that since I can no longer hope to trust you or depend on your willing co-operation, you will have to forfeit the position of leader and I will have to take command. Follow me, please."

Simon and Amity Little, immediately after their return to SWORD headquarters, had been brought to confront Warlock in the planning room where Simon had first met Warlock and his captains. The drug which had been used to subdue the Saint had been mild: he had awakened as he was being carried, his hands tied behind him, from the garage to the main building. Now he stood, his hands still tied, with Amity beside him, and listened to a grim Warlock flanked by a much grimmer Simeon Monk and Nero Jones.

"Go on," Jones growled, pointing to a side door.

Warlock had already turned and was leading the way. Beyond the elegantly panelled conference room was a grey concrete stairwell leading down into the cellar. Simon and Amity followed Warlock past an open door of heavy metal, while their guards brought up the rear.

"It's the SWORD laboratory!" Amity gasped. "It really is!"

Confronted suddenly with a huge underground chamber gleaming with electronic equipment, she sounded more amazed than frightened. Warlock's pride began to get the upper hand over his chagrin at the attempted escape.

"Reproduced exactly," he said. "It's all just as you described it, Mr Klein . . . all the marvellous devices created in your fertile brain."

Simon bowed slightly.

"My fertile brain is flattered."

"I'm sorry my reason for bringing you down here has to be what it is," Warlock continued. "If we had managed through mutual co-operation to keep our relationship on a more friendly basis, the purpose of this little tour would have been much happier for all of us." He shrugged. "As it is, I hope it will be—what shall we call it?—educational."

Warlock left the group at the doorway and walked across the room. Along the walls were panels thick with switches, dials, and varicoloured lights. One section seemed to involve a radar screen, another resembled a chemical laboratory, with retorts, tubes, and bottles. There were a number of fancifully shaped devices which resembled nothing Simon had ever seen before, and there were, unfortunately, several others which he recognized only too easily. Those latter, which would have been recalled shudderingly by any Charles Lake fan, were specifically intended for the torment and eventual destruction of human beings. One was basically electrical, one used acids in gruesomely imaginative ways, while the third, which promised a particularly messy result, operated on plain old-fashioned mechanical principles.

"How does it feel to see your brain children right here in front of you, Mr Klein?" Warlock asked.

Simon looked at Amity Little before answering.

"It makes me feel like a depraved bloodthirsty maniac," he said. "Anybody who could think up things like that deserves the acid needles."

Warlock smiled.

"I'm glad you can still laugh at yourself, Mr Klein. Luckily for you, our organization can't get along without your mind. Miss Little, come over here, please."

Amity didn't move. Warlock was standing beside a table supported by a single thick ceramic pedestal. Its surface was formed of a massive steel slab larger than an ordinary door. There was a pair of metal clasps anchored by short chains at either end of the slab.

"Come on, Miss Little."

Amity stared in wide-eyed panic at Simon. Aside from his natural desire not to see her hurt, the Saint knew that under threat of torture she couldn't be expected to keep her identity as the real and indispensable Amos Klein a secret.

"Wait a minute, Warlock," he said. "There's no need for any rough stuff. I'll work with you. I don't have any choice."

"No, you don't have any choice," Warlock replied. "And here are my conditions: that you come up with a detailed and workable plan for robbing Hermetico within forty-eight hours. Naturally, that time limit doesn't allow for any more escape attempts."

"Naturally," Simon said. "But it's still not long enough. I can't do it."

"You can, and you will. Otherwise Miss Little goes on this table—and your own future won't be any brighter."

The Saint became thoughtful.

"If I could see Hermetico, it might be possible."

"See it in person?" Warlock asked.

"Yes."

"Considering your behaviour tonight, that's an almost laughable proposition. Besides, you have the model."

"And the plans," put in Nero Jones.

"It's not enough," Simon argued. "I wouldn't even write a book based on that kind of secondhand information, much less plan a real job. I always visit any place I'm writing about, and if you'll remember the Bank of England scheme you've based this Hermetico thing on, there were several visits necessary."

Warlock rubbed his jowls meditatively.

"It's true," he said, "there were visits in the book. I believe in sticking to the book, but . . ."

"It's necessary," Simon insisted. "I'd have told you that this afternoon if I hadn't been planning to escape tonight."

"So now you'll just try to escape if we take you to look at Hermetico."

"You want your prisoner's word of honour?" asked the Saint.

Warlock returned his slightly mocking look with a cynical smile.

"I'm afraid in this day and age most of us have learned not to put much faith in honour. I put much more faith in the fact that if you are at Hermetico, Miss Little will be a hostage here. And how would you propose we get into the place for our tour of inspection?"

"The same way it was done in the book: impersonating foreign diplomats who are considering making some large and mysterious deposit in the vaults. We'll show up pretending our secretary had made all the arrangements in advance . . . or better still you could actually make the arrangements. Then we'd be sure of getting in."

"I'm impatient," Warlock said. "We'll just go there and act confused and indignant when they're not expecting us—just as it happened in your book."

"But can you come up with some authentic-looking identification papers?"

"Of course. SWORD can arrange anything. The papers will be ready in time for us to make the visit this morning before noon."

"This morning?" Simon asked.

"It's 2:00 a.m. now, Mr Klein. You've kept us up late."

"Then shall we get some sleep?" suggested the Saint.

"Not before I impress you with what will happen if you try to escape again. Miss Little, over here."

"Now, wait a minute," Simon began.

He stepped forward, but Monk caught his arm with all the gentle finesse of the pincers of a giant crane clamping down on a boulder.

"I'm not going to hurt her," Warlock said. "This will only be an edifying demonstration."

Nero Jones stepped up beside Amity and nodded towards the metal slab. Amity cast a pleading glance over her shoulder at the Saint.

"It's all right," he told her, hoping his words were true. "He's got no reason to do anything to you."

"Right," Warlock oozed.

He welcomed Amity with the unpleasant smile of a charlatan coaxing a reluctant subject onto the stage for a demonstration of hypnotism.

"Get on the table," Jones said bluntly.

"You—you shouldn't be doing this to me!" she said.

Simon admired her for not already having told them she was the real Amos Klein. He was prepared to tell the truth himself at the first sign that she was in danger.

"What are you up to, Warlock?" he asked. "I've told you I'll co-operate."

"Just a warning. Nobody gets hurt."

Amity submitted then. At Warlock's direction, she lay back on the steel table, keeping her frightened eyes on the Saint's as if even that contact with him gave her comfort.

"If you hurt her, Warlock . . ."

The Saint did not need to finish his threat. The cold, hard edge of his voice said enough. Warlock, however, did not react with any sign of uneasiness. He was like an infant fumbling eagerly with a new plaything as he pushed shut the metal rings around the girl's wrists and ankles. Amity lay spread-eagled, the short chains giving her almost no room for movement. She raised her head and looked along the length of her body to be sure that Simon was still there. He gave her an encouraging nod, which was all the help he could manage under the circumstances.

Warlock went to a control panel which sloped down from the wall at waist level a few yards from the steel slab.

"This invention of mine has several uses," he said. "Some wouldn't be understood easily by anyone without scientific training. The particular use it will be put to if you double-cross us, Mr Klein, can be understood by anybody."

Warlock pushed several buttons, and from the ceiling above the steel table something resembling a giant X-ray apparatus lowered itself with a soft hum and came to a standstill five feet above Amity's body. Its thick glass lens was like the huge protuberant eye of some Cyclopean monster from another world. The eye was surrounded by a cluster of dull black cones whose lower, smaller ends were open, pointing down at Amity.

"Are you trying to scare her to death?" Simon demanded.

"I'm trying to scare you," Warlock said. "I want you to have a vivid idea of exactly what will happen if you do anything to cause us trouble."

He moved a short lever on the sloping panel and the device which had been centred directly over Amity's body moved horizontally down the length of the table towards her feet until it was aimed at the bare surface of the slab between her ankles.

"I've combined multiple laser beams with ultra-sonic sound," Warlock went on. "The cones surrounding the laser produce the sound. In combination, focussed sound and light rays are capable of fantastic things. My friend here has great possibilities as a weapon." Warlock stroked the instrument panel as if it were a pet cat. "Of course the many ways it could incapacitate and destroy a human being are hypothetical . . . as yet. Nero, give me one of your shoes and start the accelerator."

The pale-eyed man squinted at Warlock for an instant and then grudgingly took off one of his stylishly pointed black shoes and handed it to him. As Jones then went to a second central panel, Warlock placed the shoe on the steel table between Amity Little's ankles.

"This will only be a demonstration. Don't be alarmed. Nero, please . . ."

There was a throbbing sound from the ceiling, and the device above Amity began to whine with rising pitch. Warlock fiddled with some control knobs.

"First you'll see an effect of the ultra-sonic beams, and then the laser," he said excitedly, raising his voice in order to be heard. "In real use, the table could be slowly raised in temperature until it reached a red glow. Now I'm directing all the energy only at Nero's shoe."

"Couldn't you let me up from here?" Amity called to him over the increasing sound of the machine.

Warlock, his eyes gleaming, ignored her.

"The accelerator, Nero."

Jones manipulated a larger lever, and the sound from the ceiling rose to a high-pitched scream that made the Saint's skull feel in danger of shattering.

"Now!" Warlock cried.

He plunged his finger down on a button, and there was a sound like lightning splitting the air before the deep roar of thunder. The shiny black shoe disintegrated into a heap of something like dark ash.

"The molecular bonds have been destroyed by the sound waves," shouted Warlock. "Now the multi-laser beam!"

As the turbine-like whine associated with the ultra-sonic sound abruptly faded, there was a new, throbbing noise that surged rapidly to a climax. The lights in the cellar dimmed to a candle-glow as the power apparently was sapped by the laser apparatus.

"The power of light!" Warlock exulted as he bent to press a new button. "The death ray!"

A brilliant red beam materialized between the Cyclops eye above Amity and the remains of the shoe on the table between her legs. The leather flashed like magnesium and was gone.

Within a few seconds the cellar lights were normal and all sounds had stopped coming from the machinery. The Saint saw Amity's body, which had been stiff with terror, relax as she heaved a great sigh. Warlock was laughing, all but bouncing up and down with glee. Simon looked at him with blue eyes that might have been taken from the heart of an iceberg.

"I didn't mind you so much when I could think of you as some kind of an overgrown child playing with his overgrown toys," he said in a low steady voice. "But it's a different thing when you start playing with people I like."

Warlock was still openly intoxicated with the power of his invention. His face was red and refulgent with perspiration. His jowls quivered with nervous excitement.

"Luckily your likes and dislikes aren't of much concern to me any more, Mr Klein," he shrilled. He pulled a lever and the rings which had held Amity's wrists and ankles flew open. "But your talents are very important. So go get some rest. You have two days to show us the way into Hermetico."

4

The morning was crisp and clear. Frug, in dark jacket and shiny-brimmed cap, looked as if he might have been a chauffeur all his life. The big limousine, too, looked as if it never had done duty for anything less than a general or ambassador. Its marred window had been replaced, and it bore no trace of its use in the Saint's abortive escape during the night. A small Swiss flag fluttered above one fender as Frug's gloved hands steered the big machine into a drive marked "PRIVATE—HERMETICO."

The Saint and Warlock sat in the spacious rear seat of the limousine. They were smartly dressed in dark suits. Warlock had gone so far as to affect pinstriped trousers and a white carnation in his lapel. Twin homburgs lay on both men's knees. They wore calfskin gloves.

"You make a perfect gnome of Zurich, Mr W," said Simon, "but I feel like a nitwit. Is this really the way you think diplomats dress when they go out on business before lunch?"

Warlock accepted the dig in silence. The private drive led uphill across a stony, treeless field. Ahead were fences and the low concrete dome of Hermetico's surface structure.

"You do need me," the Saint continued amiably. "Apparently your small persistent brain has been nourished on nothing but comic books and grade B movies. We'll be lucky to get out of this escapade with our lives, much less with any information about this fortress."

"Don't make any false moves and everything will be all right," Warlock said. "You know what'll happen to Miss Little if you try anything smart."

Simon looked at his companion with a despairing shake of his head.

"Even your dialogue's hopelessly corny," he said. "It's not only out of date—it's absolutely pre-war. James Cagney would feel completely at home with you."

"Be quiet," said Warlock.

Frug had pulled the limousine directly up to the main gate, ignoring instructions to park in a paved lot to the right where several dozen cars stood in rows.

"Oh, well," Simon said, settling back against the luxurious upholstery, "if we fail, we can always become a music hall comedy team."

"We won't fail," Warlock replied. "Frug, blow the horn."

Frug blew the horn twice, and then the trio in the car waited. Immediately in front of the limousine's nose was a triple-layer steel mesh gate reinforced with diagonal rods. On one side of the gate, like a guardhouse defending the smaller pedestrian entrance, which was also sealed with its own gate, was a windowless concrete kiosk about the height of a man. A sign on the larger gate said "NO ADMITTANCE TO UNAUTHORIZED PERSONS." Several other signs bore smaller print.

"The horn again, Frug."

Simon was immediately impressed with the apparent absence of all life on the other side of the wire fence, but within half a minute

Frug's honking had brought a blue-uniformed guard out of the central building and along the cement walk to the gate. There was a pistol in a holster at his hip.

"Go speak to him," Warlock told Frug. "Just as we planned—tell him we're expected."

Frug got out of the car and spoke to the guard through the gate. There was a good deal of gesturing and pointing. The guard pointed to the concrete kiosk. Frug pointed at the building. The guard pointed to the kiosk again. Frug pointed at the limousine. The guard gestured over his own shoulder at the building. Frug threw up his hands and strode back to the car. He put his head in the window.

"The guard says we've got to have passes to put in a slot in that concrete thing."

"I know that, you idiot!" Warlock said nervously. "Did you tell him we have an appointment?"

"Right, but he says people with appointments get cards to put in the slot."

"Tell him we didn't know about the cards," Simon suggested. "Tell him we've just flown into this country without publicity, and that we understood our intermediary would have made an appointment."

"Our what?" asked Frug.

"Intermediary," Simon repeated. "Tell him somebody was supposed to have made the appointment for us earlier this morning. Ask if we can speak to the manager."

"Whatever you say."

Frug went back to the gate, and a moment later the guard nodded and took a telephone from a box on the pole at the edge of the cement walk.

"He's calling," Frug told the Saint and Warlock.

"So that's what he's doing," said the Saint with bland sarcasm.

A moment later, a tall stoop-shouldered man in a grey business suit came hurriedly out of the central building and headed down the walk. Simon and Warlock stepped from the car, settled their homburgs on their heads, and went to meet him at the gate.

"My name is Thomas," the man in the grey suit said to them through the triple-layer wire mesh. "I'm the assistant manager."

There followed a lengthy interchange full of urgency, apology, and explanation. Assistant manager Thomas did not seem to doubt the identity or truthfulness of his visitors, particularly when he was given to understand that they represented a group of potential customers. They had only half a day, they said, on their way from Zurich to New York, and it would indeed be a tragedy if the stickiness of some minor bureaucratic cog interfered with a deal which—if they found Hermetico suitable to their purposes—might involve the storage of millions of pounds. They showed their credentials with the explanation that their mission must remain, for the moment, entirely confidential. They wished only to see how Hermetico facilities compared with those of its competitors. If security was as foolproof as it was reputed to be, then there could scarcely be any danger in a pair of prospective customers having a look at the premises.

The word "competitors" had a visibly stimulating effect on Mr Thomas. As soon as Simon and Warlock, as Messrs Dubray and Challons, had rested their case, he hastened to assure them that Hermetico had no competitors.

"There's no other place in the world like this one, gentlemen, as you'll see for yourselves. Of course we're delighted for prospective customers to look over the premises." Thomas reached inside his jacket and produced two red plastic cards the size of ordinary playing cards. "Each of you put one of these in the slot there on the gate control station, then come right in."

The Saint and Warlock in turn inserted their cards in the thin mouth of the concrete kiosk, which flashed a pair of green eyes and whistled. The whistle, as printed instructions on the device explained, signalled the opening of the pedestrian gate for one person only. Automatic sensing devices would sound an alarm if two or more persons per whistle attempted to enter.

"No human guards?" Warlock asked when he and Simon had joined Thomas on the inner side of the gate. "Ezz eet poh-ssible?"

Warlock was attempting a kind of amateur play-actor's stage French accent which affected the Saint's sensitive ear like a chorus of laryngitic parrots singing in Japanese. He was amazed that Mr Thomas did not immediately cry "fake" and conjure up a troupe of police officers.

"It's quite possible," Thomas replied to Warlock's question, once he had made out the words. "Automated electronic devices can't be bribed, never sleep, never drink, and can't make mistakes. We're a thousand times safer here with our automated security system than we'd ever be surrounded by guards with machine guns. For example, I must warn you immediately not to leave this concrete path that runs from the gate to the building . . . Not that you'd very likely be tempted to hurdle the fence anyway."

Thomas was referring to a waist-high barrier of aluminium rails which lined the concrete walk on either side. The walk was like the single bridge crossing the moat between a fortress's outer defensive walls and its central structure. The moat in Hermetico's case was a thirty-foot-deep band of grass surrounding the building. The moat of grass was heavily decorated with red-lettered signs shouting "Danger!" "Do Not Leave Paved Lanes!" The only paved lane Simon could see in addition to the one on which he was walking seemed to make a circuit of the Hermetico building directly outside the building's walls. That circular walk, forming the inner limit of the grass moat, was also separated from the grass by a waist-high fence of aluminium rails.

"That must be a very high quality of grass you have," Simon said, indicating the heavily protected green strip. (His own faked accent was considerably more subtle than Warlock's.) "I have never seen such zeal for preventing people to walk on the lawn."

Thomas chuckled as he led them to the building.

"The zeal isn't to protect the grass," he said. "It's to protect the people who might walk on it."

"Wot ezz hoppen?" said Warlock.

Thomas looked puzzled.

"My associate is not gifted in languages," the Saint said apologetically. "He means to ask what takes place if one walks on the grass?"

Thomas, smiling slyly, shook his head.

"I'm afraid that has to be our secret," he said. "If you knew, however, you'd agree already that our vaults are absolutely theft-proof. Come inside, please."

A small plainly furnished antechamber was the first stop inside the building. There was a second use of red plastic cards, and then Thomas took his guests down a corridor to an elevator. Beside it was a guardroom with a glass observation window on the corridor.

"Lister," Thomas said to the uniformed man inside, "I'm taking these gentlemen down."

"Yes, sir," came Lister's voice through a grating. "Come in, please."

Lister unlocked the guardroom door from the inside and Thomas stepped forward to enter it. Warlock started to follow, but Thomas shook his head and pointed to a sign.

"Only I go in here," he explained. His voice continued to come to them through the grating after he was in the guardroom and the door was locked behind him. "It's one of our precautions. Once I'm in here, you see, I'm protected from the hall by bullet-proof glass. If by some chance you should have forced yourselves in here and been secretly holding me at gun point—as happens in so many films—you would have been found out by the guard now, since he's not allowed to release the elevator until I've had this chance to prove my freedom . . . and your innocence."

A moment later Thomas, joined by two uniformed guards whom he referred to as "Duty Key Men," emerged from the guardroom and took Simon and Warlock down the elevator.

"This is the only shaft," Thomas explained as they travelled downwards. "All the others have been filled in. This is the only means of getting below—three hundred feet beneath the surface. Now, gentlemen, would you please slip these badges onto your lapels. They'll prevent alarms from sounding. Without the badges, an intruder would never get four feet without detection. Immediately on leaving the elevator I'll have to ask you to submit to a search. If you object, all I can do is give you a look through a grille."

"Oh, no objection," Simon said quickly. "Your precautions are most impressive."

"Thank you. We're very proud of them."

Warlock merely grunted.

"This will be a brief stop, and you'll soon see the vaults," said Thomas.

The elevator's doors slid open, revealing a narrow chamber whose only other exit was a six-foot-high grille of heavy bars.

"Before we can leave here, the search," Thomas said apologetically.

The two guards carried out the frisking with tact and thoroughness. Messrs Dubray and Challons accepted the operation with good-natured and innocent calm. Having expected such a search, they had carried nothing with them that could arouse any suspicion—with one significant exception. The Saint, before leaving SWORD headquarters—as he had come to think of Warlock's house—had written a short note which, if read by Hermetico's personnel, would not only have aroused suspicion but would have given Warlock's whole scheme away. The note was concealed under the lining inside Simon's Homburg. He hoped to find a means of leaving the message behind, in Hermetico, but in such a way that it would not be read until he and Warlock were outside the gates. For Amity's sake, Simon could not do anything which would result in his and Warlock's detention. He would have to leave the note, if possible, as he was going out of the building. He was not terribly optimistic, for that matter, that he would find a means of leaving it at all.

"Now," said Thomas, when the search was completed, "we can have a look at the vaults."

The two Duty Key Men brought chains from their pockets on which were fastened several elaborately shaped pieces of metal that only distantly resembled orthodox keys. One of the guards inserted his key at the top of the grille while the other inserted his at the bottom.

"Two keys have to be used simultaneously," Thomas said. "That way, no one man can ever get through a single door."

The grille swung open and the party went through. To the left was a metal door with a small square of glass in the centre.

"That's the master security control room," Thomas explained. "There are sensing devices and alarms all over Hermetico. They're co-ordinated here. So are the defensive devices. For example, gas can be pumped through the ventilating system, knocking out intruders in a few seconds. The vault itself can be completely flooded."

"*Fantastique*," Warlock said gravely.

"And most discouraging," the Saint added.

Warlock shot him a warning look.

"Discouraging?" Thomas asked.

"To anyone idiotic enough to attempt a robbery," the Saint said suavely.

"Quite so," Thomas said.

The guardians of the keys took them through another two grilles, and then they entered the vault itself. It was a long chamber containing rows of stacked metal boxes almost as high as a man's head. The place was the size of a small auditorium. A hissing torrent of fresh air gushed from an inlet grille at the far end of the huge room. The Saint's eyes immediately fell on that grille, and he immediately knew that if Hermetico had a chink in its armour, the ventilating system must be it. He had studied the plans and the model of the place already without finding any other weakness in the defences, and he had become convinced that only the ventilation ducts offered any chance at all. Now he was more sure than ever that his conviction had been correct.

Two guards with submachine guns slung over their shoulders had appeared from among the metal storage boxes. They nodded pleasantly but kept their distance.

"You may think our precautions have been carried to the point of the ridiculous, gentlemen," Thomas said, "but I think you'll also agree that there's no safer place on earth for valuables than this."

"I am more zan sateesfied," said Warlock.

"Indubitably," said the Saint. "Just one more question, please. How do you know that my associate and myself are not imposters?"

Warlock's flinch could have been detected only by someone who was looking for it. Thomas merely shrugged.

"I suppose it's quite possible for people to gain access under false pretences, but as I said, it's obvious they could do no harm. We allow only two visitors below the surface at any one time, and what could they do against our precautions?"

"Quite," the Saint agreed.

Thomas took them back to the elevator.

"Besides, I think nothing could be a better guarantee against attempted thefts than to let potential thieves see our set-up here," he said with a confident smile. "Don't you agree?"

"*Absolutement,*" said Warlock.

At the entrance of the elevator they underwent a second swift and perfunctory search—apparently in case they had managed to slip a bar of bullion under their shirts—and then returned to the surface. A minute later they were standing outside the Hermetico building at the foot of the concrete lane which led across the grass to the main gate. The brisk wind whipped their clothes and gave Simon an excuse to hold his Homburg close against his body as his fingers worked the note he had written out of the lining. He wedged the bit of paper securely in the inner band so that its upper part would be visible to anybody picking up the hat.

"Any questions, gentlemen?" Thomas asked.

"We are quite satisfied," the Saint said.

He allowed Thomas and Warlock to go slightly ahead of him to the lane, intending to drop the hat in the shadows of the entranceway of the building. He would have left the note behind simply by dropping it in a corridor or the elevator if his every move had not been constantly under the eyes of either a guard or Thomas himself, not to mention the wary Warlock.

The dropping of the hat would be a risky last chance. If it was seen immediately, Simon could retrieve it himself. If Warlock noticed later that it was missing, Simon could feign innocence: he would have no idea where it was. If Warlock sent back to Hermetico for it, the note would (hopefully) have been found, and according to its instructions the personnel at Hermetico would return the homburg to SWORD's messenger with no hint that it had served as Simon Templar's private postal service. If the note had not been found by Hermetico, and SWORD's people found it when retrieving the hat—which was quite unlikely—Warlock's already strong distrust would just have to become a little stronger.

Simon could not lose the hat as near the threshold as he would have liked because the guard delayed closing the door. By the time there were no eyes on the Saint, Warlock and Thomas were already entering the path to the main gate, and the Saint had to stay not far behind them. He tossed the hat behind him, hoping it would skid along the cement and lodge next to the building near the door.

The Saint had chosen his moment as well as he could. If the results of his manoeuvre were far from what he expected, it was probably because the gods who take an interest in such things were in a playful mood. The wind suddenly gusted violently, caught the hat in mid-air, and tossed it above Simon's head. When he saw where it was going, which was certainly not where he had intended, he could only grab for it and shout with a certain tinge of genuine anguish, "My hat!"

Warlock and Thomas turned in time to see the Homburg flip in the wind as it arched above Simon's reach. Suddenly there was an outburst of alarm bells, klaxons, and sirens, wild and earsplitting enough to have alerted a whole city.

"Oh, no!" Thomas exclaimed.

Warlock looked panic-stricken and Simon tried to look distressed as the hat, to the cacophonous accompaniment its flight had set off, dropped towards the forbidden strip of green grass.

Before it touched the ground there was the bright flash and sharp roar of an explosion. The hat, along with several square yards of turf, disappeared, and all that was left was a shallow blackened crater.

"Oh, dear!" cried Thomas.

The alarm system was still howling and hooting and clanging away. Thomas dashed for the telephone box at the main gate and shouted into it. A few seconds later the alarms stopped. In the meantime, two guards with drawn guns had hurried out of the building and were confusedly trying to decide exactly what was wrong.

"It's all right," Thomas told them. "An accident. This gentleman's hat blew into the green strip."

Warlock was struggling to preserve some semblance of calm and a French accent.

"Eez . . . eez . . . eez eet . . ." he stammered.

"I am so sorry!" Simon exclaimed in apologetic alarm. "What is happening?"

Thomas was beginning to breathe normally. He tried to smile.

"We have a radar scanner," he said. "It warns against something like a helicopter raid. Anything moving above the height of the fence sets off the alarm . . . excluding birds, of course. It's programmed not to react to them."

"But ze explosion?" Warlock asked.

"We don't tell people, but this whole green area is crisscrossed by hundreds of invisible infra-red beams. A break in any one of them causes the mine directly below it to explode."

"Wonderful!" Simon said. "I'm sorry, though, that I could have caused . . ."

Thomas waved away the apology but made it obvious that he wished to shepherd his visitors out of the gate as soon as possible.

"Think nothing of it," he said. "I only hope that we'll be hearing from you again in due course."

"I zink we can guarantee eet," Warlock assured him. "Zank you very moch."

"Indeed yes," Simon said. "Thank you."

In the limousine Frug, who had been reading a movie magazine which was now face down on the front seat beside him, was sitting bolt upright.

"I thought you'd had it!" he said in a hushed voice.

"I just had a little accident," Simon said. "Nothing to be alarmed about."

"Not very funny, Mr Klein!" snapped Warlock. "What happened exactly?"

"My hat blew away," Simon said casually.

Both men were in the back seat of the limousine. Frug turned it around and started for the main road.

"All that because of a hat?" he asked in an awed voice.

"Because of a hat," the Saint repeated. "And if that can happen on an innocent visit, think what it will be like when you try to break in . . ."

CHAPTER FIVE:
HOW WARLOCK CONTRIBUTED
SOME SCIENCE AND ALLOWED
OTHERS TO BECOME PHYSICAL

1

Simon's remark had the effect he intended. Frug glanced nervously into the rearview mirror as he steered the limousine away from Hermetico. His thin jockey's face was taut with worry.

"This is no safe-cracking job," he said to the men behind him. "It's like a war. We'd need an army to smash into that place."

"And even then the losses would be pretty heavy," said the Saint.

Warlock's cheeks were getting blotchy.

"Stop talking nonsense, both of you!" he barked. "I give the orders, Frug, and you obey. Would I get us into this if I thought we'd fail? I've more to lose than anybody. Mr Klein is perfectly capable of planning a sound way of getting into that place. He's just trying to scare you . . . which is obviously quite easy."

"It's not planning a way to get you in that's so hard," Simon said. "It's figuring a way to get at least some of you out alive that's got me stumped."

Warlock looked at the faint, mocking smile on Simon's lips and lost his temper.

"No more of that, Klein! You'll do your job just as the rest of us will, and you'll stop trying to demoralize my men! If you don't do as I tell you, you'll have the fun of watching Nero cut up your girl friend for several days before she's even put on the laser table!"

Simon had an almost overwhelming desire to put his hands around Warlock's fat sweaty neck and squeeze off not only his flow of words but his breath and finally his last croak of life. It would have been a notable pleasure to feel that gross body shuddering through its last spasm in the grip of his fingers—but the time had not come yet. Warlock felt the Saint's thoughts, though, and read them in the crystalline blue hardness of his eyes. The fat man shrank involuntarily against his own side of the car.

"Nero has orders to start on her immediately if we're not back safely," he blurted. "And that seat you're in . . . all I have to do is push this button and it explodes with shotgun shells."

Warlock's hand was on the ashtray by his window.

"I know," Simon said with forced restraint. "I wrote the book, remember? Sort of Damocles's sword in reverse. But I don't think you can afford to give me a permanent hot seat. You need me too much."

Warlock's hand remained on the ashtray then and for the rest of the twenty-minute drive to his estate.

"I need you," he said, "but I'd kill you if you attacked me."

The Saint sat back with folded arms and admired the countryside.

"Don't worry," he said absently. "I don't need to attack you. You haven't originality enough to keep yourself alive when the going gets rough anyway."

Warlock could only sputter, and the rest of the trip took place without conversation. As soon as they had returned to SWORD headquarters, Monk and Frug escorted the Saint through the house towards his room. Galaxy Rose met them at the foot of the staircase in the big reception hall. She looked even more ravishing than usual in a scanty white blouse, a red mini-skirt, and white boots.

"What would you like for lunch?" she asked after they had exchanged greetings.

She was the kind of incorrigibly sexy woman whose hot eyes and pouting mouth made even a question like that sound positively lewd.

"You?" asked Simon politely.

She glowed with appreciation.

"That might be arranged," she replied. "With or without dressing?"

The Saint glanced meaningfully at Monk and Frug, who were standing irritably by.

"Let's not discuss these things in front of the children," he said. "We'll have a walk—and so forth—later this afternoon. In the meantime, Warlock's putting me to work. I'm afraid I'll have to settle for lobster Newburg and asparagus . . . much as I'd prefer fresh Galaxy on the half-shell."

"You promise—about this afternoon?" she asked.

"Absolutely."

She smiled happily and hurried away as Simon and his captors continued up the stairs.

"The only trouble is," he remarked, "I'm not sure she wouldn't slit my throat if Warlock told her to."

"That's for her to know and you to find out," said Monk heavily.

Frug planted a bony hand in the centre of the Saint's back and gave him a shove which almost made him stumble.

"Right," Frug snapped. "I'll slit your throat myself if you foul up this job."

Without turning Simon performed a brief but highly effective manoeuvre with his right arm which landed his elbow in the centre of Frug's lower thorax. Frug sat down abruptly on the top step, clutching his belly and chest and gagging for breath. Monk, who had understandably failed to detect the Saint's lightning back-jab, stared down at his comrade with a puzzled frown.

"What's wrong with you?" he rumbled to Frug.

Frug could only shake his head and gasp.

"He's in poor condition, obviously," Simon explained. "Can't even make it all the way upstairs without losing his breath. While he's recovering, may I go on to my room?"

"You get on to your room," Monk commanded superfluously.

He accompanied Simon down the hall as Frug regained enough breath to croak out a few curses more obscene than dire and haul himself totteringly to his feet.

"Thanks very much," Simon said to Monk as they reached his room. "And I do hope your friend will be feeling better soon."

Amity was waiting for him just inside the door.

"I saw you drive up," she said eagerly. "I'm so glad you're back!"

Simon gave her the hug she was inviting, then let her help him off with his jacket.

"I'm glad to be back," he said, "but next holiday let's go somewhere different, what do you say? I get a little bored with the same view, same people . . ."

"What happened?" Amity asked anxiously. "How did it go?"

"First, I didn't escape and leave you in the frying pan," he said.

"Thanks for that," Amity said wryly. "I realize how much more important Amos Klein is than me, and I'm grateful for any little crumb he throws my way—such as letting me stay alive another few hours."

Simon kissed her lightly.

"Don't be bitter," he said. "I think I've figured out how to crack Hermetico—a possibility anyway. So before long we'll all be rich and free and happy."

He gave her a brief summary of the morning's adventures.

Amity cast a warning look towards one of the concealed microphones.

"Care to dance?" she asked.

Simon shook his head, stretched his lean frame out in a chair, and crossed his ankles.

"No need," he said. "From here on in everything's for real. Frankly, I did have a half-hearted idea for using that visit to Hermetico as a way of trapping Warlock, but it didn't work out." The Saint looked towards a mirror behind which he suspected there was a television lens. "Relieved to hear that, Mr W?" He turned his cool blue eyes back to Amity's worried face. "So I used the trip for some genuine reconnaissance—and we'd better get down to work if Warlock's expecting to lead his gallant little band in there tomorrow night."

"He won't take us with him, I suppose?" Amity asked.

"No. We're too unreliable. He'll have to make do with some of the boys who came to him with better references. As I see it, the fewer people he takes in, the easier the job should be."

"You really are going to help him," the girl said incredulously.

"Yes, I am. Or would you prefer being served up on that rich man's barbecue grill he's got downstairs?"

Amity shuddered.

"By all means help him," she answered.

"Right," said the Saint, getting to his feet. "Most of the gold in Hermetico was probably accumulated through foreign aid usury or some other form of respectable theft, or by characters without half your personal charm, my brains, or Warlock's boyish enthusiasm. Why shouldn't we have it instead of them?"

"It's all right with me," Amity said. "How do we get it?"

Simon's answer was interrupted by the arrival of Galaxy Rose with the lunch he had ordered on his way up from the car.

"Working hard?" she asked with mild sarcasm, looking at Amity as she rolled the serving cart to the dining table.

"Doing my best," said Amity.

Galaxy turned to Simon, standing so close in front of him that he had to lean back slightly in order to avoid a more intimate contact than he thought appropriate at the time.

"Can I help?" she purred.

"May I help," Amity corrected. "Yes, you may, by serving lunch. Mr Klein and I are starving."

Amity sat down at the table and waited with an all-too pleasant expression on her face. Galaxy compressed her lips and glowered.

"I'm not your slave," she crackled. "Do it yourself."

"You're Mr Klein's slave," Amity said sweetly. "And Warlock's, too. So please do as you're told and don't keep us waiting."

Galaxy Rose clenched her fists against her thighs.

"Amos, make her stop it before I . . ."

Simon thought it wise to accept the invitation to mediate before he became ammunition in a feminine free-for-all.

"Calm down, girls. I hate being fought over at mealtimes. Anyway, I have to work."

He sat down at the dining table and proceeded to open the wine. Galaxy obediently but huffily served his and Amity's plates.

"I really could help you, Amos," she said pleadingly. "I'm sure I could do more than she could."

"I'm sure you have done more," Amity said, "but for the work Amos is doing you need something you haven't got."

"And what's that?" demanded Galaxy.

"An adult human brain."

The Saint put his napkin to his mouth, stood up quickly, and ushered Galaxy to the door. He let his hand linger on her arm.

"I'll see you about four," he said. "I'm sorry, but I do have to work now."

"On her," she said bitterly.

"On Hermetico," he replied. "Be glad you're better at playing than working. People ask much pleasanter things of you that way."

Galaxy softened perceptibly.

"We'll play later, then. Bye-bye."

Suddenly her lips touched his, and then she was gone. Amity rolled her eyes and groaned as he returned to the table.

"I wonder what school for delinquent girls Warlock dredged her out of?" she said, cracking down with unrestrained violence on a lobster claw.

Simon raised his eyebrows as he spooned some hollandaise sauce on to his asparagus.

"You and Galaxy aren't getting along so well lately, I gather."

"When did we get along? I'm just getting mightily sick of seeing her—" She interrupted herself suddenly and looked at him. "You're implying that I'm jealous, aren't you?"

"Not in the least," said the Saint gravely.

"Well, I am!" Amity said. "I'm sick of seeing her rub up against you every time she happens to pass through the same wing of the building."

Simon raised both his hands above his plate helplessly, very much aware of the omnipresent microphones and television cameras.

"I find myself in an awkward position," he said. "Flattering but very awkward, and if we use our vaunted brains, we will understand just why."

The pointed tone of his last sentence got through Amity's emotions to her reason.

"I'm sorry," she said sheepishly. "I am acting like a child." Suddenly she sounded almost on the verge of tears. "Maybe it's just the strain of . . . of not knowing . . ."

Simon touched her hand soothingly.

"The strain doesn't need to go on indefinitely," he said. "Let's concentrate on making this Hermetico job a successful operation."

Amity took a deep breath.

"You're right. It'll get my mind off myself. Tell me what you found out."

2

The Saint continued eating at a leisurely rate as he talked.

"Hermetico has some of the defects of the Maginot Line," he said. "It's too confident and it's too rigidly oriented in a single direction. The management is so sure of the power of automation that they don't watch the outer fence carefully enough. The only real problem is getting across the infra-red beams that protect the grass strip."

"The only real problem?" his companion asked dubiously.

The Saint speared another snowy chunk of lobster, coated it with sauce, and savoured it luxuriously before he answered.

"I mean it's the only real problem involved in getting from outside the fence to the inner side of the mined strip."

"And how do you propose to get from outside the building to the vault?" asked Amity.

"For that matter," said Simon cheerfully, "how do we propose to get over or through a six-foot-high network of invisible beams, any one of which will set off a mine if you interrupt it?"

"You could go over, I guess," Amity said.

She was beginning to take an interest.

"You can't go over because where the infra-red beams leave off six feet above ground there's a radar system scanning the air. Nothing larger than a bird can go above the fence without setting off alarms."

"Is there some way to get at the radar system?"

Simon thought about it.

"Not from outside. If we tried jamming it all we'd do would be to arouse suspicion and bring guards out all over the place before Warlock and his boys could even start to get over the fence."

The two of them went on eating in silence for a while. Amity pushed away the emptied shell of her lobster and stared at it thoughtfully.

"I wonder how many of those infra-red beams there are?" she mused.

"Exactly what I was thinking," said the Saint. "I noticed that even though the beams are crisscrossed up to six feet, my hat didn't hit one and set off a mine until it was just a foot or so above the ground. It was sailing in at a slight angle, too, so that must mean that there are some fairly good-sized gaps in the network. I'm sure there's no place a man could walk straight across, or even zigzag across—"

"But maybe there'd be a channel somewhere, like a tunnel several feet above the ground, where no beams happened to cross," Amity interrupted.

"It's possible," said Simon. "I'm glad to see you getting so excited."

Amity tried to change her expression abruptly.

"I'm not excited."

"Well, please get excited. Maybe you'll come up with some brilliant ideas—like how to find out if there's a channel through the beams, and how to get through it."

Those words were the beginning of an afternoon of non-stop thought, talk, and study. Amity's cigarette stubs filled an ashtray and her smoke filled the room. Plans and charts covered the floor. Notes and calculations covered the tables. The Hermetico model was all but taken apart completely and put back together again several times.

It was almost four o'clock when Simon sighed, rubbed his eyes wearily, and stretched his arms, signalling a break in the labour.

"Time for your walk?" Amity asked with only a glimmer of sarcasm.

"It's pretty obvious that the only way to the vault is the ventilation shaft," he said, ignoring the remark.

"But we're still stuck with those damn infra-red beams," Amity sighed. "If only we could see them or something, then we could . . ."

"Wonderful!" Simon said.

"What?" she inquired blankly.

"Wonderful. See them. You've got it. With the right equipment we could see the beams. Something as simple as a pair of Polaroid glasses with a coating of . . . what would it be?"

"Something sensitive to infra-red light, you mean?" exclaimed Amity. "Exactly. But what?"

Simon looked up towards the ceiling and pressed his palms together in a prayerful attitude.

"Oh mighty Warlock," he intoned. "Hast thou some elixir sensitive to infra-red light lying about the place?"

With an answering buzz the panel which covered the television screen was already drawing back. The screen flickered to life with the image of Warlock's eager round face.

"It might really work!" came his excited voice from the loudspeaker.

Simon stood and salaamed.

"Thou hast heard, oh All Knowing!"

"I'll get to work on it immediately," Warlock said. "I'll have you brought down as soon as we're ready for a test."

Warlock was on his way out of the picture even before the screen had become completely blank. There was a knock at the door of Simon's room.

"So soon?" Amity said.

"It is time for my walk," Simon said. "Why don't you get some rest?"

"I'd much rather join the fun and games out on the greensward," Amity said as Galaxy walked in.

"You can't both go out at the same time," Galaxy said promptly. "Anyway, three's a crowd."

"Better a crowd than your company," Amity retorted. She had gone to the open door of her room. "Well, Amos darling, bring 'em back alive . . . the clichés, I mean."

"What is she talking about?" Galaxy asked.

The Saint walked with her down the corridor.

"Don't worry about it. Amity has a very intricate mind."

"And I'm stupid, I suppose?"

"If you sometimes give that impression—which you don't, of course—I'm sure it's because nobody can believe anybody with your beauty could also have a brilliant mind—which you do, of course."

"Well, I never had the chances she did. That's obvious."

"It's a good excuse, anyway."

Galaxy looked at him with sudden irritation. They had just come out onto the front steps of SWORD headquarters. Simon continued walking until he and Galaxy were out of range of the microphones which were hidden all over the building. He didn't doubt that there were other means of monitoring his conversation even out in the garden, but he knew that in moving about constantly in the open he was at least interfering with the clarity of reception.

"What do you mean—excuse?" Galaxy asked him.

"I mean that saying you never had a chance is just a way of evading responsibility for yourself. When you can blame everything on bad luck or whatever you want to call it, you've got a perfect excuse for just floating with the tide. There's nothing Amity can do that you can't do. I'm sure of that."

She slipped her arm under his and walked close beside him as he strolled towards the relative privacy of a few beeches near the wall that surrounded Warlock's property. The sun was low, reddening as it descended towards the horizon through a cloudless sky, and shadows were long on the carefully tended grass. In such pleasant circumstances, the Saint felt almost guilty for lying to Galaxy about her limited intellectual potential.

"I haven't done so bad," she said cosily. "I've got lots of nice things, and I'll have lots more after tomorrow night. And look who I'm with."

"And look where we are," Simon said wryly.

He made a sweeping gesture to indicate the wall. Galaxy pressed against him reassuringly as they stopped beneath the beech trees.

"Don't worry," she said. "Everything will be all right after tomorrow night."

"At least I won't have to worry," the Saint said grimly. "I'll be dead."

"Dead?" she exclaimed.

"You don't think Warlock will let me or Amity stay alive to tell the world what he's done, do you?"

"I don't care about Amity. I wish he would kill her. But he won't hurt you. I'm sure he won't."

She sounded more hopeful than convinced, and Simon seized the opportunity.

"You know as well as I do that he'll have to kill me," he said urgently.

"No! He's . . . he's not the type."

He took her in his arms and whispered in her ear.

"I'm sure they can hear what we're saying even now, so don't talk out loud. Pretend I'm kissing you."

She shivered and clung to him.

"Why pretend?" she whispered.

Her lips were suddenly against his, and it was several minutes before either of them spoke again.

"Galaxy," he said in ardent tones which would have quickened the pulse of a Hollywood film director, "if we ever get out of this thing, I'm going to take you away someplace and spend about six months making sure we both forget it."

"Oh, Amos, I'm so glad . . . You can write your books, and I'll . . . I'll . . ."

"Do what you're best at," he suggested.

She giggled against his shoulder.

"Yes."

Simon straightened and assumed a tragic expression.

"But there's no use talking about it. I won't be alive, and Warlock would never let you go."

"I could go," she said indignantly. "I'm not his slave."

The Saint looked her in the eye.

"Are you sure? I have a feeling none of you are here just out of sheer love and loyalty to dear old Warlock. And I don't think it's just the profit motive, either. What's he got on you?"

"Got on me?" she asked nervously.

"Yes, got on you. What's the hook he's holding you with? I've got to know that before I can risk too much. Were you in prison?"

"No! There wasn't enough evidence."

"But there would be enough evidence to convict you if Warlock spoke up to the police? Is that the idea?"

"Something like that," she said coldly. "Does it matter? Lots of people get killed in wars all the time, and nobody thinks a thing about it, but just let one person get rid of somebody's nagging bitch of a wife in a way that doesn't even hurt at all and you'd think the world was coming to an end!"

Simon's aplomb was put to the test which, of course, it passed nobly.

"You performed this good deed, I take it, with the husband's permission?"

"I . . ." Galaxy caught herself and looked at him wisely. "I never said I performed anything," she went on. "But this husband—the way he acted when she was dead—you never would have known the whole idea was his." Galaxy disgustedly broke a twig from a bush next to her. "Men are such cowards."

"What happened to him?" Simon asked.

"He died too. Not long after." Galaxy smirked. "Of a broken heart."

"More likely of a highly spiced steak and kidney pie," said the Saint. "And Warlock is going to share your old family recipe with the police if you don't co-operate?"

"Even if you're right, it doesn't matter," Galaxy insisted. "I'm glad I'm here anyway. Who wouldn't be, for the money I'm going to get?"

Any romance Simon had been able to instill into the moment had been pretty thoroughly dissipated, but he tried to restore a little of it as he drew Galaxy closer to him again.

"Listen," he whispered. "I have plenty of money of my own. If we can get out of here alive, you can have anything you've dreamed of . . . and the money's in my bank account, not in Hermetico."

"I couldn't. Not if you mean before Warlock gets back tomorrow night."

"That's what I mean," Simon said urgently. "We'll have to escape tomorrow night while they're at Hermetico."

Galaxy was shaking her head and trying to draw back.

"Who's we?" she asked sceptically. "I suppose she's supposed to go with us."

"She's going as far as the other side of the wall anyway. We can't leave her here. But then. . ."

"But then nothing!" Galaxy said. "Men are all liars." Her expression changed suddenly. "Unless . . . we got rid of her. Then I'd know you were serious."

Simon was quickly calculating the possible advantage of pretending to agree to Amity's liquidation until Galaxy had given him the means of escape, and then turning the tables.

"Then you'd help me get out of here tomorrow night?" he asked.

"Oh, no. I'm waiting for my share of the money. I'll be sure you get out after that, and tomorrow night we'll get rid of her. Right?"

Simon shook his head, abandoning the whole project.

"No. We're not getting rid of Amity. If you do get rid of her Warlock will be upset and . . ."

"We could make it look like she was trying to escape. Or she was sick. That's the way I . . . it was done to that woman before. Warlock has all kinds of chemicals. He lived in the flat next door to me at the time . . ."

"And you borrowed some of his potions."

"Something like that," Galaxy said proudly. "I've watched him. I could get something that would make it look like Amity just suddenly . . ."

"No," Simon said firmly. "If you killed her, I . . . I'd feel too guilty to go away with you anywhere."

Galaxy stepped back and gave her whole body a jerk like an enraged child.

"You're just like the others!" she said. "Men are all talk! I know what you'd do. You'd let me get you and her out of here and then you'd throw me over so fast I wouldn't know what hit me!"

The Saint was grateful to see Bishop appear by the corner of the house at that point and call to him.

"Mr Klein! Warlock would like you to come to the laboratory!"

"Right away," Simon replied. "Sorry, Galaxy. We'll have to continue this pleasant chat later."

She hurried along close beside him as he strode across the lawn to the front door.

"If you let me get rid of her I still might believe you," she said. "Then I'd know you were serious."

"No," said Simon. "That's absolutely out."

The details of Galaxy's subsequent remarks would be of interest only to a serious specialist in colourful English colloquialisms.

"Come along quickly, please," Bishop said at the door, and led Simon and Galaxy to the cellar.

Warlock was standing beside one of his lab tables painting a small square of glass with a greenish metallic liquid. On the table was something like a sun lamp with a focussing lens in front of it. Frug stood nearby watching.

"Ah, Klein!" Warlock said. "Just in time. Frug, plug that cord in, would you?"

Frug plugged the lamp-like device into a wall outlet. Warlock flicked a switch.

"There," he said with satisfaction.

"Is it on?" Bishop asked. "I can't see anything."

"Of course you can't," Warlock said impatiently. "Infra-red radiation is like light, except that it's beyond the range the human eye is designed to pick up. If we could see it, do you think we'd be going to all this trouble?"

Bishop looked uncomfortable, and his head seemed to sink lower than usual between his shoulders. Simon raised the piece of coated glass to his eye and turned to the table on which the infra-red device sat. Where a second before he had seen nothing, he now saw a distinct beam of pale light. He nodded, and Warlock took the glass with such excitement that he almost dropped it on the floor.

"It works!" he exulted. "We've done it. Klein, you're a genius."

"I know," Simon said humbly.

"Now we can get in Hermetico?" Frug asked.

"Not necessarily," Simon told him. "But you'll at least be able to see the beams that may blow you to bits."

Warlock compressed his lips and gave Simon a stern look.

"I've asked you to stop your discouraging talk," he said. "Tell us the rest of your plan."

"There isn't any rest yet," the Saint said. "I'd suggest you send somebody over to Hermetico right away with a piece of this glass—or better still with several pairs of glasses coated with this stuff—and give it a test."

"But we already know it works," Frug interrupted.

Warlock turned to him in nervous exasperation.

"Will you go back to your ridiculous magazines?" he snapped. "It's better than having you interfering at every turn!"

"I have another reason for sending somebody over there," Simon put in. "We need to know how thickly those beams are interlaced. It won't do you any good to see them if there's not enough space between them anywhere for you to work your way through."

"Is that clear to you, Bishop?" Warlock asked. "As soon as I've coated some glasses, you and Nero get over there and do as Mr Klein said. I'll give you some ideas on estimating the distance between beams. There's a wooded patch that comes near the fence at the back of the Hermetico building. It's the only place where you can get quite near without being seen. For heaven's sake don't let anyone spot you."

"Just one other thing," Simon said. "If it's possible to make a circuit of the whole fence without getting caught, try to see if there's a channel through the beams."

"Right," Warlock agreed. "But since the pattern of beams will probably be the same all the way around, don't take any risks. Now go get Nero and explain everything to him. I'll give you the glasses on your way out."

"And shall I go back to my palatial cell?" Simon asked.

Frug was still hovering near the door as Bishop left.

"You're not gone yet!" Warlock snapped at him. "Take Mr Klein to his room." The next words were directed to Simon. "You're doing a fine job. If there's space among the beams, we can either walk through or make an aluminium extension bridge to put through any channel. Have you worked out the details of getting to the vault through the ventilation system?"

"Not completely. I won't have it finished before tomorrow sometime."

"Good. We'll plan to enter Hermetico after midnight tomorrow. Shall I tell you what Bishop and Nero have found out when they come back tonight?"

"I'd rather get some sleep," Simon said. "I think I can control my excitement."

"Understandable. You were a busy fellow last night. Which reminds me, Mr Klein . . ."

Simon had started to walk out into the corridor. He turned in the doorway.

"What?"

"If you have any intention of building some trap for us into your Hermetico scheme—don't be foolish enough to think I won't detect it. After all, I've plenty of time to study the plans too, and I'm as familiar with the place as you are—probably more so."

"I'll keep that in mind," Simon said.

"Good. If you forget, the consequences could be most painful . . . for you, not for us."

3

Remembering Warlock's words early the next afternoon, the Saint silently pondered the fact that the consequences of a slip-up in the Hermetico raid could be most painful for everybody concerned—Warlock included. And it was a slip-up he counted on to end the career of SWORD and its leader. But at the same time he was vividly aware, without Warlock's needing to warn him, of the folly of trying to include a trap for the raiders in his and Amity's plan for the theft. Warlock was no stupid man by any standards. He would undoubtedly spot the weak point in the scheme, keep the main part of the plan for immediate use, and simply eliminate the weakness and the two people who had conceived it.

Simon had no intention of being eliminated, but he had every expectation that Warlock would fall into a trap. Hermetico itself, even with no help from the Saint, was a trap. The chances of a party of men entering the place and leaving it without being detected—even with the best laid of plans—were approximately those of a party of arthritic rabbits making their way undisturbed through a kennel of greyhounds.

There were too many unpredictable elements. Merely getting the van (which would be necessary for transporting men and equipment, and later for removing the stolen metals) near the fence and leaving it there during the raid involved a tremendous risk of detection, even if Hermetico did not feel the need for human guards around the periphery. More importantly, Bishop's and Jones's check on the infrared beams had revealed that while there were gaps through which men might enter, they were several feet in the air and so small that the slightest error would break a beam and set off an explosion.

Those problems were just the beginning. At any step a dozen different and deadly things could go wrong. The Saint felt sure that SWORD's expedition would fail quite easily enough on its own, without any special help from him. If Warlock was too much of a nut to see that, all the better.

"I suppose that's it," Simon said to Amity. "We've finished."

He turned from the window of his room, from which he had been watching Monk complete the repair to the front gate Simon had wrecked two nights before. Amity was sitting at the worktable with a small dormant volcano of cigarette remains at her elbow and a pencil behind one ear. She was chewing a thumbnail and staring at one of the maps of Hermetico's innards.

"We still don't know if there's some kind of detection device inside the ventilation duct," she said.

"We've done the best we can," Simon answered. "We can't be expected to know more than we could possibly know. What happens now is up to Warlock."

Amity tilted her head to listen.

"What's that?" she asked.

She and Simon went to the window and watched a van move from behind the garage, where it had been parked since its arrival in the morning (Bishop had apparently gone out and bought or rented it), into the drive. A few hours before it had been a big bright thing of shiny aluminium. Now it was painted a dull, non-reflective black. Frug and Bishop opened its back doors, manipulated something inside, and an aluminium ladder-like projection moved horizontally straight out behind the van until it extended over twenty feet. Warlock came out of the front door of the building to watch as a pair of legs were automatically lowered from the extended end of the projection, forming a kind of bridge supported at one end by the truck and at the other by the legs.

"That's what they'll try to get through the beams on," the Saint said.

"Go across it, Bishop," Warlock called.

The bridge was about a foot wide and equipped with continuous parallel rows of rollers. To move along it, Bishop, starting at the truck, had only to lie on his large belly and scoot along the rollers like a seal on ice. In a few seconds he was at the outer end.

"Don't flap your arms about like that while you're crossing or you'll blow us all to kingdom come!" cried Warlock. "And we can't have the thing sagging like that in the middle."

The leader went over to the contrivance and inspected it in detail, gave some inaudible orders, and as he turned back towards the house saw Simon and Amity at the window.

"Have you finished?" he asked from below their vantage point.

"Almost," Simon told him. "We'd like to make a final check before I hand over the plan."

"Good!" Warlock called back. "That's fast work, Mr Klein. I've got together all the equipment you suggested. You can give the whole group a briefing when you're ready. We'll meet in the planning room."

Warlock went into the house. While her and Simon's heads were still out of the window, Amity whispered to him.

"Isn't there anything we can do to stop this?" she asked.

"I think Hermetico will stop them," Simon replied. "Our best bet is to worry about escaping from here while most of them are gone tonight. I might even be able to follow them to Hermetico and be sure their plans get upset."

"What do you think he'll do to us if we don't escape?"

"I don't know . . . and I don't like not knowing."

The van was being moved back behind the garage. Only a few more seconds of whispers beyond the windowsill would be possible.

"How do we escape?" Amity asked.

"If you have any ideas, we'll dance." Simon let his voice rise back to normal as he pulled his head into the room. "We'll deserve a celebration after all this work."

Simon waited until four o'clock to call for the SWORD briefing. Half an hour later he and Amity were accompanied down to the planning room by Monk and Nero Jones; Monk carried the Hermetico model and Jones carried an armload of papers and rolled maps. In the oak-panelled meeting room Warlock and Bishop and Frug were waiting. A blackboard was set up at one end of the long table. Reddish afternoon sun streamed in through the high windows.

When everyone was seated at the table, Warlock stood and addressed them.

"You are all aware that what we are undertaking tonight is one of the most difficult tasks a group of men have ever risked their lives to accomplish—but the rewards are worth the risk. After the work of this one night none of us will ever need to work again. Of course SWORD deserves to go on, and I hope we—or some of us—will be together on other adventures. However, no one will need to work, so those who want to can reasonably think of tonight as the gateway to an easy and luxurious future."

Simon, who had no inclination to listen scornfully to praise of adventures and luxurious futures—two things he looked forward to confidently himself—nevertheless was amused by Warlock's blithe propaganda. It set the tone perfectly for his own lecture which was to follow. The Saint's plan was to radiate confidence and happy enthusiasm about the whole Hermetico scheme. The less guarded and apprehensive the raiders were, the more likely they were to run into trouble. Simon would mention only the more cheerful prospects, underplaying the dangers and not referring to certain pitfalls that had occurred to him as possibilities which he had somehow failed to include in the plans he was presenting to SWORD.

Warlock was continuing his sanguine speech, looking from one face to another.

"I've heard you all talk about your ambitions. Now's the time to keep them in mind. Frug can have that stable of racehorses now. Nero can buy that wicked night club. Bishop can have his yacht. Monk can even have his harem, I suppose."

There was nervous laughter around the table. Nero Jones licked his pale lips. Frug was clasping his hands so tightly in front of him that his fingers were like white knobby icicles.

"And now, Mr Klein . . ."

Simon stood up on cue and went to the head of the table. The plans lay in front of him and the blackboard was behind him.

"You all know already how you're going to get through the fence and the infra-red beams. There'll be no problem as long as everybody does his job properly. Judging from the view from my window, the bridge you've made works like a charm. The truck will back up to the fence, then Frug will cut the hole, taking precautions to avoid the alarm going off when the mesh is clipped."

Using the blackboard for illustrative sketches, the Saint showed them how that would be done. He described in detail the extension of the aluminium bridge through the barrier of infra-red beams to the walkway which surrounded the building.

"The circular walk, directly next to the building itself, is unprotected," he said confidently. "The designers seem to have felt that nobody would ever be able to force his way through the fence and the infra-red mine field. Their next really strong line of defence doesn't come until the bottom of the elevator shaft—which we plan to bypass completely."

The Saint held up a chart of the surface area of Hermetico.

"Briefly, when you've crossed the bridge, you go around to the left until you come to these two large ventilators. One is the intake and one is the extractor. The fan of the extractor is above the surface here, in the neck of the duct. You'll cut the duct right at the ground level, below the fan, without severing the wiring . . ."

Warlock held up his hand politely.

"The key to the operation," he interrupted, "is not to disconnect anything that might set off an alarm."

"Right," said the Saint. "But there's nothing to worry about, really, since we've pinpointed all the danger spots already. In case an alarm should be set off, Nero will be staked out with a machine gun covering the front door. He should be able to keep the opposition inside until you can get away to the van."

"What about other doors?" Bishop asked uneasily.

"There's only one other door, here on the left side. You'll pass it on your way to the ventilators. From where Nero will be, he can get an angle on both doors. Remember, this place was built strictly with defence in mind. It's made to withstand bombs and full-scale invasions. There's just no way for the defenders to get out and mount an offensive."

Bishop and the others looked satisfied, and Warlock looked downright smug. It was Simon's own business if he did not share their lack of respect for Hermetico's architect. The defenders did not need to mount an offensive. A close study of the plans had led him to believe that a series of very small square openings around the upper part of the dome of the otherwise windowless structure were intended for use as gunports. The guards could lay down a deadly barrage without leaving the protection of the building. They could not see the area immediately next to the building but anything near and beyond the perimeter of the outer fence was at their mercy.

"After the ventilator is opened," Simon continued, "Frug will be lowered down it on a harness. He'll arrive at the main vault, which he'll be able to see through a large grating. He'll knock out the two guards who're stationed in the vault by shooting them with drugged darts. Then he'll take off the grating and Bishop will join him in the vault. The object then is simply to take over the whole place. Using keys they'll take from the vault guards, Frug and Bishop will get out of the vault and make a sneak attack on the control centre. Then they can shut down the alarm system, and the rest of you can simply walk in the front door . . ."

Frug did not look at all pleased with the plan.

"Why not just hoist the gold and stuff up the ventilator shaft?" he asked.

"We thought of that," Simon answered. "But the vault is three hundred feet down, and you'd spend all night getting out just a fraction of the loot . . . assuming you had all night, and nobody discovered you in the vault. I think you'll be much safer getting command of Hermetico in one quick stroke, then using their facilities for moving the heavy stuff up to the van."

Warlock nodded approvingly.

"It's true," he said. "It's the only way."

"It is unless you're just after a few souvenirs," the Saint added. "As I understand it, you intend to empty the place."

"Exactly," said Warlock.

Bishop was wriggling in his chair.

"What about guards up top?" he asked.

"There'll probably be one in a booth by the elevator on the ground floor," Simon said. "But before he knows you're in the building you'll have taken control of the alarm and defence system, so it shouldn't be much of a problem to handle him. We can go into details about all these things in a minute. There's also a sleeping room for guards just off the entrance alcove. Probably there'll be half a dozen men in there. The Hermetico defence plan seems to depend almost entirely on automatic devices for warnings of trouble. Most of the guards can sleep, since they don't actually have to stand guard, but they do constitute a kind of defence force that can be called on by automatic or manual alarms at any second."

The conference went on for over an hour and then, when Simon had answered every objection and explained every detail of the operation, moved to the basement laboratory and store rooms. There, for another hour, Warlock's men brought together various pieces of equipment and discussed and tested them. Warlock, having followed the formation of the Saint's and Amity's plan on television, had foreseen most of the needs of the expedition and made certain they were on hand earlier in the day.

"Everything seems to be in order," he said finally. "We'll eat in a while and get some rest. Then we'll have some rehearsals with the equipment at nine o'clock before we load it in the van. The last thing we'll do is test all the weapons. We'll leave for Hermetico before midnight."

"And what do we do?" Amity muttered to Simon in the midst of the clatter and talk at the meeting's end.

"We'll just relax here with our window open and listen for explosions off in the direction of Hermetico . . ."

4

But for once the Saint underestimated fate's fondness for involving him in adventure—in this case adventure within adventure. He was not to be allowed to sit quietly in his room listening for the explosive demise of Warlock and his doughty band, nor even to spend the night engineering his own and Amity's escape from SWORD headquarters. An explosion took place, and it involved Warlock, but it occurred in Simon's own room.

He and Amity were at the dining table finishing off their meal with fresh cherries and peaches when the door burst open and Warlock sailed towards them like an apoplectic dirigible.

"Well, Mr Simon Templar!" he shouted.

He was waving a magazine, but the dramatic effect of his entrance and gestures was ruined by the fact that he had begun to quiver all over. Simon looked at him with bland puzzlement.

"I thought you were rehearsing a raid, not *Uncle Tom's Cabin*," he said.

Frug and Nero Jones flanked Warlock menacingly. Galaxy stood triumphantly behind them. The magazine appeared several inches in front of the Saint's nose.

"Try to talk your way out of that!" Warlock bellowed.

"Try to hold it steady enough for me to see," the Saint replied mildly.

He took the magazine and saw what he expected to see: his own picture.

"Well?" Warlock shouted.

"Very handsome," said the Saint.

He glanced at the cover of the magazine. It was one of those sensational movie journals with which Frug was occasionally seen enriching his mind. The magazine was two weeks old, and it had a spread on the then forthcoming premiere of Amos Klein's *Sunburst Five*. Under Simon's picture—taken during his attendance at some other gala occasion he could no longer remember—were the words:

> *Real life Charles Lake expected at premiere. Simon*
> *Templar—better known as the Saint—is among those*
> *invited. Don't shove, girls! You might find a date with him*
> *about as relaxing as a ride on a tiger shark . . . and he's*
> *not talking about his romantic enthusiasm. The legendary*
> *Robin Hood of Modern Crime has probably survived more*
> *narrow escapes than even Charles Lake.*

"Well?" Warlock demanded again.

"The prose is lousy and the quote's a pure fiction. Otherwise . . ."

He shrugged and passed the magazine to Amity.

"You tricked me!" Warlock raged.

"You kidnapped me," said the Saint.

"You let me believe you were Amos Klein. You insinuated yourself into my organization—probably with the intention of destroying it. You haven't succeeded yet, and you won't! I'll see you both dead for this!"

Nero Jones looked excited by Warlock's last statement, and his fingers caressed some solid object in his jacket pocket. Amity Little put the movie magazine on the table.

"What have we done?" she asked. "Except to try to go along with your crazy ideas?"

"And who are you?" Warlock asked her furiously.

"You wouldn't believe me," she said.

"An accomplice," Warlock stormed. "Otherwise why would you have co-operated in this masquerade?"

Simon had been thinking at racecourse speed, and he had decided that the best way to protect Amity was to let Warlock know her true identity.

"In spite of your archaic diction, I think you have a brain under those layers of baby fat and romanticism, so I'll let you in on something," Simon said to the tremulous Warlock. "This lady is Amos Klein."

Warlock's safety valve went with a wheeze of rage, and his square hand swung towards Simon's face. The Saint did not move from his casual position in the chair. With a slight tilt of his head he avoided Warlock's slap, caught the square hand, continued its motion further than its owner had anticipated, and sent Warlock sprawling on his face on the carpet.

The solid object which Nero Jones had been handling so affectionately inside his pocket openly revealed itself as a snub-nosed revolver, and Frug snapped out a six-inch switchblade. Simon did not move except to shake his head warningly at Amity as Warlock floundered first to his knees and then to his feet.

"You'll pay for that too," he said, his face livid with fury. "For tripping me and for insulting me with idiotic lies about this . . . this woman of yours!"

"But it's true," Amity said. "I wrote the Charles Lake books. My real name is Amity Little, but my pen name is Amos Klein."

"So you see," Simon joined in, "SWORD got a real bargain. Two brilliant experts on crime for the price of one." He gave Warlock a winning smile. "We aren't even charging you double. For a mere hundred thousand pounds you're getting not only a master plan for cracking Hermetico, but also the delightful company of two celebrities in your own home. Why, you'll be the envy of the neighbourhood, Warlock, old son of a witch."

The man who called himself Warlock, surprisingly, did not erupt again. Instead, a strange unnatural calm regained control of his quivering bulk that was far more ominous and blood-chilling than any of his outbursts. It reminded the Saint suddenly and startlingly that the house and the organization around him, the whole set-up and everything that had gone before, preposterous and fantastic as they were, were not figments of delirium but had been put together with cold and patient practicality.

"You're right," he said at last, slowly. "I have your plan and I'm going to use it . . . and you're coming along as insurance. In case you've included any traps, you'll be the first to die, so you might as well admit anything you've deliberately done to try to catch us."

"You have as many facts about Hermetico and the plan as I have," Simon said. "Do you think Amos and I included any traps?"

"No. I don't think you were that foolhardy, and that's why I'm not calling off the raid. But just in case, you will come with us. Your . . . Miss Little or whatever she is will be clamped on the laser table downstairs and won't be let up until we get back. If you betray us at Hermetico and we don't arrive back here by a certain time Miss Little will die. Is that clear?"

"She actually is Amos Klein," Simon said. "You wouldn't want to destroy the person you admire most in the world, would you? I don't blame you for being sceptical, but you could at least check."

"I don't care any more," Warlock said icily. "And just to be sure you take me seriously . . . Frug."

Warlock nodded towards Amity, and Frug and Nero advanced on her. She backed away. When Simon made a move to put himself in front of her, Warlock pulled a dart pistol from his pocket.

"I can put you to sleep in a second, Mr Templar—and my aim is good. Stand still."

As Simon watched helplessly, Frug caught Amity by one of her arms, swung her around, jerked her arm up behind her, and held the point of his knife against the side of her throat so that the skin was pressed in but not quite punctured. Amity winced with pain, and Frug twisted her arm even more viciously.

"Nero is very interested in women," Warlock oozed. "His interests are a bit odd, but for that reason I suppose they'll furnish us more entertainment."

Nero, standing in front of Amity, had put his pistol away and taken a cigarette lighter from his pocket. He flicked it into flame with slow deliberation, looking Amity in the eye all the time. It was one of those lighters meant for use on pipes, with a control that could turn the flame into a sideways jet like a miniature blowtorch. He demonstrated it, making the jet lick out and in like a small hot tongue. As it approached her eyes, he suddenly took it away and laughed. With his free hand he reached forward, caught the collar of her blouse, and ripped it half open. Now the coal of the lighter moved with taunting slowness towards the white swell of one of her breasts. She tried to wriggle away, but Frug held her, increasing the twisting pressure on her arm. Her face blanched and her eyes closed. The tip of the flame seemed to just touch her flesh and then Warlock intervened.

"That's enough for now. Mr Templar should have the idea. Galaxy, take her downstairs and put her on the table. Nero will help."

Nero reluctantly released his hold on Amity's blouse and withdrew the lighter. She gasped with relief as Frug relaxed his grip on her arm and shoved her towards Galaxy. Galaxy caught her by the shoulder and tried to swing her roughly towards the door, but at that point Amity performed a turn-about entirely worthy of the creator of Charles Lake. As she pretended to stumble forward she caught Galaxy's wrist in both hands, jerked her off balance, and in the same swift flowing motion threw her sprawling heavily on her back several yards away.

"It's all right," she said quickly to Warlock as he raised his dart pistol. "I'll go peacefully. I just had to get that out of my system."

"Bravo," said Simon.

"Take her downstairs, boys," Warlock said. "Clamp her to the table. Galaxy will have orders to give her the full treatment, if we're not back from Hermetico by a reasonable hour."

Galaxy was in no shape to take any orders at the moment. She was still on the floor, dazedly wondering what had happened.

"Is all this clear to you, Mr Templar?" Warlock asked.

"I'm afraid it's very clear," Simon replied.

Frug and Nero were escorting Amity though the door to the hall.

"Good luck," she said to Simon over her shoulder.

Her voice was unsteady but controlled.

"Don't worry," the Saint called after her. "It'll be all right."

"It had better be," Warlock said soberly. "It had certainly better be. Now come along, Simon Templar, and get ready to prove that your plan really works."

CHAPTER SIX:
HOW HERMETICO WAS BREACHED AND SIMON TEMPLAR DID NOT HAVE THE LAST WORD

1

The expedition was ready to leave SWORD headquarters at one o'clock in the morning. Warlock was fuming over delays and shouting at his men as they gathered in the reception hall. Warlock and Bishop wore police uniforms, and the others—including Simon—wore black trousers and long-sleeved black sweaters. It was hoped that if the raid was interrupted, Bishop and Warlock might be able to pass themselves off as policemen who were in the process of apprehending and taking away the criminals.

"All of you except Monk go out to the truck," Warlock commanded. "Go over the equipment checklist completely and test everything again. Mr Simon Templar and I are going down to see that his lady love is comfortable. Monk, you come with us."

As Simon followed Warlock to the cellar, with Monk guarding the rear of the little procession, the rest of the men trooped silently out the front door.

"I think you might need some last-minute inspiration, Mr Templar," Warlock said. "Go in, please."

The Saint entered the cellar and saw Amity lying spread-eagled on the steel table, her ankles and wrists chained. Galaxy was lounging in a swivel chair eating chocolates and reading a vividly coloured paperback called *Holiday Lust Spree*. Amity raised her head and tried to smile at Simon as Warlock shot Galaxy an angry look.

"Must you read that trash? If you can't pay attention to what you're doing here, you could at least try improving your mind."

"Assuming she has any mind to begin with," Amity said.

Galaxy called her several names which even the author of *Holiday Lust Spree* would have been forced to delete from his manuscript.

"If we're not back by three-thirty," Warlock said, "you are to turn on this machine and eliminate Miss Little slowly but completely."

"With pleasure!" Galaxy said.

"Isn't that early?" Simon asked. "We could hardly be back by then anyway."

"Of course we can," Warlock said. "It's five past one now. The trip to Hermetico takes twenty minutes. We'll be there at one-thirty. I allow until two o'clock for us to have opened the building, and until three o'clock at the very latest to complete the loading. We'll easily be here by three-thirty." He smiled grimly at Amity's helpless figure. "And besides I'm sure Galaxy won't get the thing over with too fast. Even if we were five minutes late—which I guarantee we won't be—there'd still be something left of Miss Little to save. Admittedly, the ultra-sonic waves would have destroyed that mind she seems to be so proud of, but her body would be quite intact."

Amity lost her surface composure. She closed her eyes and lay back on the slab with a heavy shuddering sigh. Simon started to move towards her, but Monk intervened.

"No, Mr Templar," Warlock said. "No fond farewells. Concentrate instead on being sure of a reunion."

"All right then," the Saint replied icily. "Let's not waste any more time. Try to relax, Amity."

"Good luck," she said.

"If you've got any ideas about starting to work on her before three-thirty, I promise to fix your face so that even dogs will run away from the sight of it."

"Not very gallant of you, Mr Templar," Warlock said, as Galaxy merely gaped like a spoiled child whose hand has just been slapped for the first time. "Galaxy will obey her orders to the letter. And so will you. Let's go."

Five minutes later the van rolled out of the gates of Warlock's grounds. Behind came the counterfeit police car; Bishop drove it, Simon sat next to him, and Warlock and Frug sat watchfully in the back seat. The pace was slow, and a winding route along back roads towards the rear of the Hermetico building necessitated considerable caution and flashing of brake lights on the part of Monk, who was driving the van. But at that hour of the night there was little traffic, and within the twenty minutes specified by Warlock they had reached the pasture they would have to cross in order to reach their goal, which was still half a mile away.

Nero Jones jumped from the van, clipped the wires of the low fence, and waved his arm to signal Monk to proceed. The van bounced slowly through the opening and rumbled off across the rocky field with Nero back inside. Ahead, as the police car followed, Simon could see the patch of forest which was their goal. There was no moon, but the sky was clear, and even though both the vehicles had turned off their lights the bright masses of stars gave a silvery illumination of the whole landscape which disposed of any problem about finding the way.

Warlock was leaning forward tensely, looking at the van.

"Why is the fool tearing along like that?" he fretted. "He'll turn over."

"He's only going ten miles an hour," Bishop said.

"Mind that rock!"

"I see it," said Bishop.

A sulky cow plodded leisurely out of the way as the procession growled through its hitherto private territory. Warlock, taken by surprise, had yanked out his automatic before he realized the bovine nature of the lumbering shape.

"Good idea," Simon said. "Work in a little big-game hunting and we'll have steaks for breakfast."

The cow gave a belligerent moo as it was left behind. Warlock snorted and shoved his pistol back under his coat.

"We're coming up to the wood now," he said. "Everybody be set to go."

"I still don't get why they don't have lights all around the place," Frug said.

"So if anybody decided to drop a bomb on it from a plane at night he wouldn't have an easy time spotting it," Simon answered.

"Oh, sure," Frug sneered disdainfully. "Drop a bomb on it!"

"It could happen," Warlock said. "This place is built to be completely safe even in war. Tend to your own business and don't jabber so much."

"At least none of us is nervous," the Saint observed amiably.

"Shut up!" Warlock croaked. "Where are they? Where's Monk off to?"

"In the trees," Bishop replied.

The van had disappeared into the darkness of the forest, and the police car followed slowly. The shadows shut out most of the light of the sky, making it difficult to see anything.

"Keep up, then!" Warlock commanded. "Don't lose them entirely!"

Suddenly the van loomed directly ahead of the police car, moving in reverse. Warlock waved his arms and fired off a broadside of orders.

"Stop! Watch out! Don't run into him! Pull alongside!"

He rolled down his window and called harshly to Monk in the driver's seat.

"What the devil do you think you're doing? You're going backwards!"

He was beginning to sound like an elderly schoolmarm in charge of her first picnic outing for juvenile delinquents, and yet that incongruity only lent an additional spine-chilling quality to the reality of what was happening.

"I know," Monk said, not bothering to hold his voice down. "We've got to turn around here and back up to the fence!"

"Quiet!" Warlock ordered furiously. "You think you're at a football match? Turn around, then. How far are we from the fence?"

"Not far. Fifty yards."

"Back up and give them room, Bishop," Warlock said.

The van grunted laboriously to and fro among the trees, and then moved very slowly in reverse in the direction it had originally been travelling.

"We'll stop here," Warlock said when the police car had followed another hundred feet. "Come along, Mr Templar, and no tricks. I don't need to remind you . . ."

"No," Simon interrupted. "You don't."

"Bishop, hurry on up and help them," Warlock ordered. "We'll follow. Do you have your dart gun, Frug?"

"Check," said Frug, crisply, slapping a bulge in his jacket.

"It is just like a movie, isn't it?" Simon commented.

Bishop had already disappeared ahead. Warlock and Frug got out of the car and waited for the Saint to precede them.

"Hurry it up," Warlock said, "and no more comments."

Monk and Nero Jones were already at work on Hermetico's outer fence when Simon, Warlock, and Frug came around the van to join them. Bishop was inside the van adjusting the exact height of the aluminum bridge to match that of the hole his colleagues were making in the fence. For the first time since his involuntary joining of SWORD, Simon was impressed with the professionalism of Warlock's group. They went about their assigned tasks as quickly, quietly, and efficiently as those automatic electrical devices of which Warlock was so fond. It was as if real ability lay coiled inside their unimpressive personalities, to be released only in the rare moments when it was needed for a specific job.

"Careful," Warlock said unnecessarily to Jones. "One slip with those jumper leads and all hell will break loose."

Monk grunted and went on clipping through the fence as Jones bridged the gaps with wires which would prevent circuits from being broken and setting off an alarm. Simon scanned the scene around them. The big pale dome of the building itself, like the upper third of a monstrous tennis ball, rose not thirty feet away. From this rear view it was unlighted and almost completely featureless. It might have been made of solid rock, a fallen moon dimly reflecting the light of the night sky. Around the outside of the fence were signs illuminated by hooded bulbs; they warned in unspecific but emphatic terms of the dreadful fate which awaited anyone attempting to transgress on Hermetico's premises.

The hole in the fence was complete. It was over three feet in diameter and about three feet above the ground level at its lower edge. Frug was passing around spectacles coated with the chemical that Warlock had provided. Simon put on his pair. Instantly the dark area between fence and white building was alive with bars of light, crisscrossing one another from earth to the top of the fence.

"Good work," said Warlock.

He was looking through the hole in the fence along the tunnel which his men had found in the network of rays. It was not a very spacious tunnel, and it was not of uniform dimensions all the way through, but it was big enough for a prone man.

"The bridge," Warlock grunted.

He motioned to Monk, who went into the cab of the van and backed it up until the open rear doors were within a foot of the fence. The engine of the van, which had been muffled by every means Warlock could contrive, still seemed as loud as the racket of a sawmill.

"What if somebody looks out here?" Frug muttered.

"We're all dead," Simon assured him.

"Shut up!" Warlock hissed. "Nobody's going to look out. There aren't any windows."

Simon glanced hopefully at the tiny apertures around the upper part of the dome—scarcely visible except to one who was looking for them—and said nothing.

"Now," Jones whispered, and Bishop pushed the lever which moved the bridge out from the rear of the van.

"Easy," Warlock said. "Slowly. Easy does it now."

The metal projection crept from the cavity of the van and nosed through the hole in the fence. It inched its way down the tunnel, precariously close to the irregularly spaced bands of light which formed the channel. Simon, like the others, felt compelled to stand as close to the bridge as he could and sight along it as it moved out across the deadly mine field. No one breathed. The night wind rustled the trees behind them. The sound of the electric motor which moved the vibrating bridge was a low whine in the background.

"Stop!" Warlock barked suddenly.

The head of the bridge had almost touched one of the beams. There was an adjustment within the van. The bridge crept on. Simon was almost touching it. With a sudden shove he could have set off explosions all across the green strip, but his chances of standing up to or even just escaping Warlock and his men, single-handedly and without a weapon, were infinitesimal. He would have to wait until the group had split up inside Hermetico's grounds before he could make his move.

As the far end of the bridge reached the other side of the ray field there was a general intake of breath. A switch was thrown inside the van, and the two legs which were to support the suspended end of the bridge eased towards the ground just next to the concrete walk which surrounded the outside of the dome.

"Are you sure it's steady on those supports?" Warlock whispered.

The others were sighting along the aluminium frame.

"I can't see a bloody thing," Monk grumbled.

"What if it's not steady?" Frug asked. "It'll swing over or something and blow us all to pieces."

"Not all of us," Warlock said shrewdly. "Just one of us. Let's see the famous Saint demonstrate his talents. You go across first, Mr Templar, and make certain that the bridge is in good shape. And please notice that when you get to the other side there's absolutely nowhere for you to run in case you should have any lingering ideas about causing trouble. Nero and Frug will both have guns trained on you the whole time. They could finish you in two seconds. Now, go ahead. If anything feels wrong to you, stop."

"Everything feels wrong to me," Simon replied. "Is that all the information you need?"

"Get on the bridge, Mr Templar."

The Saint mounted the rear of the van, looked down the narrow tunnel of darkness among the web of light rays, and lowered his body onto the track of metal rollers.

2

He felt the aluminium bridge shudder slightly, almost touching one of the light beams. But then there was a scraping creak as one of the legs on the far end adjusted its contact with the ground, and the whole frail structure steadied itself.

"Go on, Templar," Warlock urged. "Remember what happens to your girl friend if we're not finished here on time."

Simon held his legs close together, extended his arms straight before him, and without further hesitation used the full strength of his fingers to pull himself quickly along the rollers. He slipped smoothly past the fence and out through the silent unwavering network of infra-red beams. A few seconds later his head and shoulders emerged from the wall of rays, and the rest of his body followed. He gratefully lowered himself back to solid support in the form of the cement walk which circled Hermetico's dome.

Looking back, he saw that Bishop was ready to follow, making himself prone on the aluminium rollers at the edge of the truck bed. Down to the right about thirty feet was Nero Jones with a submachine gun strapped to his back and an automatic rifle aimed directly at the

Saint. Frug, a few yards along the fence from the other side of the truck, covered Simon with a smaller automatic weapon. Even if he should make the bridge collapse by kicking away the supports with his feet, getting rid of a man or two with the resultant explosions, the Saint knew that he would be instantly cut down by Frug's and Jones's interlocking fire.

Such a move would accomplish nothing but the salvation of Hermetico's treasures for Hermetico's management and depositors—none of whom were uppermost in Simon's mind at the moment. He was considerably more interested in squaring accounts with Warlock and his friends, and in the process saving himself and Amity Little. He would have to wait. In the meantime, he surreptitiously tried to weaken the stance of one of the bridge's supporting legs by kicking it with his foot as he moved away from it. If the bridge should fall down while he was nowhere near it, who could blame him?

But unfortunately the support moved only a fraction of an inch. Bishop's weight was already on the bridge. With a long canvas pack ahead of him on the rollers, he was inching out over the mine field.

"Elbows in," Warlock said hoarsely. "Don't raise your head."

Whatever Bishop's qualifications as an extra-legal professional man, he was obviously not very good at or very fond of crossing shaky aluminium bridges over highly explosive strips of earth. When he finally had both feet planted on the ground beside the Saint his face gleamed with sweat in the starlight and his hands were trembling visibly.

"Come on now," he said condescendingly to the ones who still had the crossing to make, "there's nothing to it."

Across the bridge in slow procession came Monk, then Warlock, and finally Frug. With them they brought more canvas packs, the metal tanks which would fuel the acetylene torch, and a great coil of nylon rope.

"Legs together," Warlock grated to Frug. "Easy does it, you idiot! Don't drop the rope!"

Frug's reaction to the crossing was more vehement than Bishop's had been. He mopped his face with his sweater and swore.

"I wasn't half an inch from one of those beams at the end! Will I be glad to see those bloody things shut off!"

The sooner we get below, the sooner they'll be shut off," Warlock said. "Move out now—around to the ventilation ducts."

There was a muffled clanking as Monk shouldered the metal tanks.

"Quiet, you fool!" Frug squeaked.

"Who d'you think you're calling a fool!" Monk rumbled.

"Shut up, both of you!" Warlock said. "Do you jobs and don't think about anything else." He faced back towards the outer fence and whispered to Nero Jones as they passed his position. "Get to your post now. Don't fire unless you're absolutely sure something is wrong."

Jones waved acknowledgement and headed off across the field, circling the outer fence parallel to the circle the rest of the group was making around the dome. He would post himself a hundred feet beyond the fence at a spot from which he could fire either on the side door or the front door of the Hermetico building. His pale face was an eerie circle of white when he glanced back over the shoulder of his black sweater. It had not occurred to anyone except the Saint that Jones should smear his face with blacking in order to camouflage it, and the Saint had somehow neglected to mention the idea.

"Get a move on," Warlock said. "You can't see anything with those glasses over your eyes now, Frug. All of you, get them off."

Only Simon kept his glasses on. He pushed them down on his nose so that he could have a choice of seeing over them or through them. It was one of his more optimistic hopes that there were uncharted and unexpected infra-red beams within the confines of Hermetico itself. If that turned out to be the case, he would be the only one to see them. The SWORD group was so engrossed in its work that none of its members gave the least thought to the spectacles propped on the end of Simon's nose.

Bishop and Frug led the way. Simon came next, with Monk and Warlock behind. They walked swiftly but quietly in single file around the featureless sloping wall of the building. The only sounds were the night breeze, the muffled clanking of the equipment the men carried, and the cautious scuff of their feet. Then there was a new noise which grew louder as they continued—a low buzzing roar.

"Those are the ducts up ahead," Warlock said. "Easy does it."

They had circled far enough around the building for the van to be out of sight. Then, as the roaring of the ventilation ducts grew louder, Simon discovered that his infra-red sensitive glasses served their purpose sooner than he had hoped. The SWORD group was passing the side door of the Hermetico building, the only door beside the main entrance: it was made of riveted steel plate, undoubtedly bomb-proof, and it was recessed into the concrete wall of the dome. What interested the Saint about it was that he saw—and was the only one of the party who could see—a single beam of infra-red light crossing the threshold six inches above the ground. It was like a rope stretched across the entrance to trip an intruder who might step into the recess in an effort to open the door—except of course that instead of tripping anybody it would set off an explosion or an alarm or something equally inhospitable to an unsuspecting trespasser.

Unfortunately that door was not included in SWORD's plans, but Simon decided he would find a way to see that it was included. He would have to act, though, before the men who were entering the vault through one of the ventilation ducts had managed to seize the control room and shut off all the electronic defence mechanisms.

A few yards past the doorway, like the roaring heads of subterranean monsters, were the ventilator ducts. The extractor duct was marked by the great bulge of the fan in its throat. The fan which drew in air through the other duct was below ground, incorporated into a filter system which prevented gas being used to knock out Hermetico's human defences.

"Here," Warlock said. "Gather around. Quickly! Get that torch going."

Monk and Bishop assembled the acetylene apparatus with silent efficiency. Warlock knelt by the extractor duct and drew his finger across the metal a few inches above the concrete base.

"Cut here," he said. "The wires run down just below that part of the fan. Be sure you leave them intact."

"Huddle round now, would you?" Monk said. "Cut down the glare."

He was referring to the light of the acetylene torch. The other men stood close by as the point of Monk's flame cut into the duct at the place Warlock had indicated. The metal was thick, and the work went slowly. Simon relaxed his muscles by deliberate effort and thought the situation over. It would be two o'clock before the duct was open, and even if everything went well down below for the raiders it would be two-thirty before the loading of the van could get well under way. Warlock undoubtedly would see that the loading was completed as rapidly as possible, and that his patrol car got back to his headquarters in time to stop the killing of Amity . . . if he really intended to stop it.

The irony was that by disrupting SWORD's operation Simon might cause such delays—to himself included—that Amity might die directly because of him. On the other hand, the Saint did not believe that his or Amity's chances of a long and happy life would be particularly improved if they depended on Warlock's mercy, which, he was now convinced, did not drop as the gentle rain from heaven. The Saint would have to act, and sooner than he had hoped. He had originally thought he would wait until the loading was under way, assuming the theft got that far; now he decided it would be more sensible to bring confusion to SWORD's ranks while one was outside the fence, two were below ground with no way of getting out, and only two were with Simon on the surface.

Warlock was perspiring heavily as the cutting of the duct continued, even though he was involved in none of the labour.

"Can't you hurry it up?" he snapped.

"The thing's made of bloody armour plate," Monk grunted. "I'll be done in a minute."

The last part of the cutting was the most delicate. A small part had to be untouched, so that the wiring which led up from below to the huge fan would not be severed. The instant Monk gave the go-ahead, the whole group joined in carefully lifting the head of the duct and laying it back on the concrete, where the fan continued to roar.

Frug had already strapped a leather harness around his waist and chest. One end of the nylon rope was attached to the harness. Bishop was clamping a frictionless roller to the jagged edge of raw metal on the lip of the duct.

"All right, Frug, over you go," said Warlock. "Let him down gently, boys. Have those sleep-darts ready, Frug."

Simon peered down into the duct as he took a hold on the rope. Three hundred feet below he could make out a smudge of light: the illumination of the vault coming through the outlet grille.

Frug disappeared down the great dark throat like a fly descending into a bassoon.

"Easy does it," Warlock mumbled. "Don't bounce him about down there. Mustn't have any noise."

After some time a section of the taut rope marked with red tape passed through Simon's hands.

"There's the warning," whispered Bishop. "He's almost there."

"Steady now." Warlock let the other three men support the weight on the rope while he felt the strand like a doctor testing a patient's pulse.

"Now, lower away a fraction of an inch at a time. Stop immediately when I feel the tug . . . A bit more . . . Now, stop!"

Frug had signalled that he was in position behind the grille, which gave his sight and his dart gun access to the vault. Motionless, the men at the surface waited. They could hear nothing but the roar of the fan beside them, and like fishermen they poured all their consciousness into their sense of touch to judge by slight pulls on the line what was happening far below.

At last there were three definite jerks on the rope, which meant that Frug had knocked out the vault guards and would be removing the grille while the rope and harness were drawn back up for use in Bishop's descent. The line went slack and as Bishop and Monk hauled it up Simon took one last look around through his coated glasses and inconspicuously removed them. He was going to try to make use of the infra-red beam across the recessed doorway after all, and he did not want the glasses to arouse suspicion.

A moment later, Bishop was in harness and ready for his descent. Simon was ready too. The next few minutes would contain that precise instant in which he alone would take fate in his hand and twist it to his own will . . . or else find that fate was not so flexible, and that its revenge for such a challenge was death.

3

The Saint estimated the amount of rope being fed down into the duct with Bishop dangling at the end of it. This time there was less tense caution in the operation and more haste. Frug would not quite have taken the grille off the mouth of the duct by now. Bishop was about a hundred feet from the bottom.

"Wait!" Simon whispered suddenly.

He froze, looking towards the rear of the building. Monk and Warlock froze too, their eyes wide. Bishop was left temporarily suspended in the duct.

"What is it?" Warlock breathed.

"Somebody there?" asked Monk.

"I thought I saw somebody," the Saint answered.

"If you're trying to . . ." Warlock began.

"I'm not trying to do anything, but I don't fancy getting shot standing here like a goat on a tether. Shall I go look?"

"Oh, no, you don't!" Warlock growled. "You and Monk hang on here."

Simon smiled underneath the grim expression he had to keep like a mask on his face. He felt like a chess player who has just set up his unsuspecting opponent for an inescapable forking trap: in denying Simon the chance to leave the rope, a chance Simon would gladly have accepted, Warlock had opened himself to an equally catastrophic possibility.

"Stick close to the wall," Simon cautioned.

Warlock had drawn his pistol. He edged along the side of the dome, keeping his back close against it. The recessed doorway was only a few feet ahead of him. He stopped and looked back, shaking his head as if ready to call off his search. Simon urged him on with desperate motions of his own head. Warlock moved further along the wall. When he was directly outside the recessed door, the Saint struck.

"Look out!" he shouted.

Warlock stumbled back into the doorway in a panic-stricken dive for cover. Instantly there was a tumultuous clamour of bells and sirens. Even Simon, who was expecting the uproar, and possibly worse, felt something like a galvanic shock from the tip of his tongue to his toes. Monk very nearly jumped straight in the air, though his fingers automatically clung to the rope.

Warlock was staggering from the doorway, coughing, rubbing his eyes wildly with one hand as he waved his pistol with the other. A thin mist was spraying from around the locked steel door, apparently a gas meant to blind and otherwise incapacitate a would-be intruder temporarily.

"Help me!" was the most Warlock could manage to cry as he stumbled against the railing, almost into the mine field, and then back towards the wall of the building.

Monk's eyes were gigantic with surprise and fear, and he stood as if he had suddenly been frozen solid, his huge hands clinging numbly to the rope.

"What is it? What is it?" he croaked.

"Time you were left holding the bag," Simon answered.

He released his own grip on the rope and threw himself towards Warlock. The fat man, still blinded and having lost all sense of direction, was standing with his broad back towards the ventilation ducts. The target was too tempting to resist, particularly when every second was vital. The Saint hurled himself like a wrestler catapulting the full weight of his body off the ropes at his opponent. His right shoulder smashed into the centre of Warlock's back and sent him sprawling on his face. The pistol which was Simon's main goal scooted from Warlock's hand across the concrete walk and three feet out onto the grass at the edge of the mine field. Since it touched no infra-red beams it set off no explosion, but in order to get it Simon would have had to prostrate himself on the walkway and stretch his arm carefully under the low beams.

He did not have time even to consider that possibility, for within a second or two after Warlock hit the pavement a new and chilling sound joined the howl of sirens and clanging of bells. It was Bishop's shriek of helpless horror as he plummeted down the duct like a stone.

Simon whirled from Warlock's floundering form to see Monk, his hands free, lurch towards him from the beheaded extractor vent. The tail end of the rope was uncoiling rapidly from the ground and disappearing over the edge of the vent's mouth. Bishop's agonized cry, just before it was suddenly cut short, was joined by a brief and quickly truncated squawk from Frug, who had apparently been unable to get out into the vault in time to avoid breaking his comrade's fall.

The Saint dodged and ducked as Monk's arm swung at him with all the weight of an oak log. He chopped the huge man in the kidneys and sent him reeling against the wall of the building. But Monk, however much like a clumsy gorilla he might look at other times, proved surprisingly agile when fighting for his life. Without a second's delay he rebounded from the wall and got off a left and a right jab at Simon, either of which could have taken off the head of a marble statue if it had landed squarely. But the Saint managed to counter the left and take the right on his shoulder. Now he was knocked back to the wall, and Monk dived at him. Simon rolled aside, yanked Monk's wrist, and swung him heavily against the concrete dome.

Even that failed to slow down Monk, who lunged at Simon, withstood a tremendous smash to his jaw, and lifted the Saint completely from the ground with a crushing bear hug. Monk's aim was clear: he intended using the momentum of his charge to carry the Saint to the mouth of the extractor vent and hurl him down the hole. The Saint, however, had no intention of being thrown down the hole. Monk's dependence on his own brute strength made him forget to guard himself against more subtle forms of attack. Simon slashed out with his forearm, slicing so hard into Monk's larynx that the grip of the huge arms was loosened immediately as Monk fell choking and gagging to his knees.

In the instant which passed as he drew back his foot to swing the toe of his shoe against Monk's jaw, the Saint had time to realize consciously what the new sound was which had joined the general cacophony. Nero Jones's machine gun had opened up out beyond the fences with a chattering blast. Simon assumed at first that Jones was firing at guards who were trying to make a foray out of Hermetico's front door, but then he realized that the machine gun was aimed at him. The next staccato of explosions sent lead gnawing into the cement wall not six inches above his head.

He had to forego the pleasure of kicking Simeon Monk in the face, and instead drop to his own knees. Monk lunged at him, knocking him onto his back with the sheer force of his weight. But the impetus of Monk's weight served another purpose: it enabled the Saint to catch the gigantic man in the pelvis with both feet and flip him completely over his own body. Monk landed with the small of his back on the rough metal edge of the open extractor vent down which he had dropped Bishop. His legs were in the three-hundred-foot-deep shaft before he could catch himself. For an instant the back of his sweater, snagged on the jagged metal, delayed his complete disappearance down the duct.

"Stop me!" he screamed.

But the sweater ripped free, Monk's head dropped suddenly from sight, and the prolonged sound of his wild howl echoed from far down inside the earth.

Nero Jones's machine gun ripped into the wall by Simon's shoulder. Stony chips and dust shattered from the face of the dome, stinging his eyes and nostrils. The Saint had hoped the Hermetico guards would have opened the side door by now, but obviously their strategy did not involve exposing themselves to bullets when they could remain safely inside their fortress. There was a roar of gunfire from high up in the dome as they began to answer Jones's fusillades.

There was absolutely no shelter along the side of the dome. Simon knew that his only chance to avoid being cut down was to get back across the aluminium bridge. He picked up his glasses, which had been knocked to the ground, and tensed himself low on his knees for the dash. In his path was Warlock, who had thrown himself on his stomach and was groping out over the edge of the mine field to recover his pistol. He obviously had regained most of his sight.

He screeched to the Saint, "You bloody fool! You've ruined everything! It was working! It was perfect!"

Simon ran, leaping over Warlock, racing for the bridge. Lead barked at his heels and whistled around his head. A glance over his shoulder told him that Warlock had retrieved his pistol and was staggering to his feet. He was crazed beyond all caution, screaming incoherent curses as he pitched forward into a stumbling, weaving pursuit of the Saint.

Simon reached the bridge. At least for the moment he was beyond Nero Jones's angle of fire, but he knew the respite was only momentary. He had glimpsed Jones's white face bobbing in the darkness of the field. The machine-gunner was on the run himself. He too was heading for the escape car, and in a few seconds he would again be in a position to fire at the Saint. Luckily, the guards in the dome were still concentrating on Jones, giving Simon at least some chance of getting across the bridge to shelter without being noticed immediately.

He shoved the coated glasses back on his nose as he ran and without a moment's hesitation more or less dived onto the rollers of the bridge, launching himself like a torpedo so that he shot along the aluminium rails and was almost to the other side before even the most alert gunman could have reacted to his appearance and taken aim.

Simon was pulling himself the last feet of the way to the truck with powerful clutches of his fingers when he heard Warlock shouting hysterically behind him. The pistol cracked twice, undoubtedly aimed in the Saint's general direction, but without any more effect than Warlock's words. Then, incredibly, he felt a violent shaking of the bridge.

"Damn you!" Warlock was crying. "I'll get you! Nobody beats Warlock! It has to be like the book! It's real!"

Simon could not raise his head to see the man, who was trying to kick the supporting legs from under the inner end of the bridge. But Warlock had arrived too late. Simon was already rolling through the fence into the dark protection of the van.

It was only then that Warlock seemed to recover his reason enough to realize that he was kicking down his own means of escape. He clambered onto the bridge, his arms stretched in front of him along the rollers, his pistol aimed at the van. He fired even as he dragged himself along, and the bullet ripped up through the roof of the van.

Suddenly a voice more like the voice of a machine than a man resounded from a loudspeaker within the wall of the dome.

"Halt there or we'll shoot! Give yourselves up. You have no way of escape."

Warlock floundered along the rollers with greater urgency.

"Don't shoot," he screamed. "Don't shoot me!"

"Halt!" bellowed the loudspeaker.

Warlock stopped midway across the bridge, clutching the rails desperately even as he took aim against Simon.

"I've stopped! Don't shoot!"

That was when Simon moved his foot to push the lever which controlled the bridge. Slowly the electric motor began to draw in the rails. The supporting legs at the far end grated and creaked. Warlock, as he realized what was happening, squirmed and bellowed. His eyes rolled wildly as he clawed at the rails and tried to haul himself forward.

Then the already precarious support of the metal legs gave way, and the bridge tilted and sagged. Through his glasses Simon could see Warlock roll with flailing arms into the web of light beams—the last, almost immaterial wisps of reality with which Warlock would ever have to deal.

A series of explosions erupted across the mine field with a volcanic thunder that buried all other sound. Simon dived for the floor of the van as he saw the bridge blasted into flying, twisted shreds. Stone, turf, and metal rained down on the van's roof and onto Simon's back. Then, the instant the rain of debris ended, he rolled over and swung himself to the ground, taking advantage of the cloud of smoke and dust which enveloped the whole area to make a dash into the woods. He could only hope that Nero Jones had not managed to get to the car ahead of him.

4

As Simon raced around the van into the dense wood, an unworldly silence suddenly replaced the bedlam of bells, sirens, gunfire, and explosions. Hermetico's alarm system had been shut off, and there was nothing left in sight for the guards to shoot at. The only sound the Saint heard behind him now were the distant muffled sounds of Hermetico personnel.

He hurried on stealthily into the darkness of the wood, straining his eyes to try to see whether or not the police car was still parked in the clearing where it had been left. It was, and there was no sign of Nero Jones, who easily could have made it back to the car before Simon. Either Jones had been shot by the guards from their posts in the dome, or he had come to the car, found that it had no key, and escaped on foot.

But there are ways of starting cars without keys, so it was most likely that Jones had been hit by the withering fire from Hermetico before he ever got to the trees. The Saint quickened his stride to a run. The luminous dial of his watch told him it was ten minutes before three. Every step of the operation had taken longer than anyone had foreseen. Still, if he could start the police car Simon knew he could get back to Warlock's estate before the three-thirty deadline.

Then to his right he saw a smear of white weaving irregularly among the black tree trunks. Almost immediately there was a sputtering flash of pale fire from directly beneath the bobbing white smear, and the silence was blasted by the voice of Nero Jones's tommy gun.

The Saint's nearest protection was the police car itself, which was far from being the ideal sanctuary, since once he had reached it there was nowhere else to go, but at the moment he was delighted to put it between himself and Jones's bullets. As he squatted by the rear wheel he heard the lead pellets shattering glass and ripping into metal on the other side.

Nero Jones obviously had been wounded as he crossed the open field on his way to the wood. During a break in the fire, Simon hazarded a glance around the rear of the car and saw his enemy standing slumped against a tree at the edge of the clearing, completely careless of the target he himself was presenting. Since he could not know that Simon was unarmed, it was apparent that Jones was in such a bad way that he scarcely knew what he was doing.

With that in mind, the Saint tried something he might otherwise have hesitated to risk. His peek around the back of the car had brought on another blast from the tommy gun. A few seconds later, hearing nothing more from Jones's direction, he deliberately exposed his head and shoulders again. Jones was limping cautiously forward from the trees. He fired from the hip, seeming barely able to support the weight of the gun. Simon screamed in mock pain, stiffened to his full height with his hands clutching his head, and fell back out of Jones's sight again behind the car.

Even as he went through his performance, he managed to get a glimpse of the wounded man coming forward at a staggering run. Simon rolled under the car and watched Jones's feet approach until they were within a dozen inches of the door. The shoes were splattered with blood. Nero Jones could scarcely drag himself forward. Simon felt liquid spreading over his own lower leg and wondered fleetingly whether he had been hit without realizing it. But he had no time to wonder now. He thrust himself from under the car and grabbed both of Nero Jones's ankles, jerking both his feet completely out from under him.

Jones crashed over backwards, his shoulders and head striking the ground first. Simon had already clutched the barrel of the tommy gun. He wrenched it from Nero Jones's hands, raised himself on his knees, and without bothering to turn the weapon around to firing position, swung it as a club. The stock smashed against Jones's skull. He shuddered and lay still.

Simon, still on his knees, caught a deep breath. Jones would never exercise his skill as a torturer of women again, and as much credit went to Hermetico's guards as to the Saint. The albino's chest had been torn open by rifle fire, one of his arms was drenched with blood, and the flesh of one of his legs had been hit by several bullets.

Jones's wounds reminded Simon of the moisture he had felt on his own leg. He quickly checked, and what he found made his heart sink. He would almost have preferred finding his own blood. His trousers were soaked with gasoline. He lay flat again and confirmed that the police car's gas tank had been shot through and by now was completely empty.

Simon got to his feet and looked closely at his watch. It was six minutes before three. He had no chance at all of getting back to SWORD headquarters in time to save Amity if he walked to some paved road and tried to get whatever transportation he could from there. There was only one way he might get to her in time, and that was by taking the van which was still parked next to the Hermetico fence. The odds were in favour of there being a key in the ignition switch, since the van's electrical system had powered the aluminium bridge, and Simon knew that the rear of the van had not been seriously damaged in the explosion which had killed Warlock. The gas tank was safely forward near the engine.

Sirens were wailing in the distance, growing louder. The police were on the road to Hermetico—or maybe they were reinforcements for police who had already arrived. Whatever the situation, Simon had no intention of saving his own skin by running—which he easily could have done—and leaving Amity to be slowly broiled by Galaxy Rose. He grasped the tommy gun in firing position and ran back through the wood towards the van.

There were several things in his favour. The Hermetico guards' primary responsibility was the defence of the vault. By coming out of the building and giving chase to intruders they might play into the hands of a clever enemy.

The sounds of gunfire continuing to come from the wood had probably given them additional reason for caution, otherwise they could easily have been swarming around Warlock's police car before this. The Saint could assume that they were still inside Hermetico, waiting for the police to search the surrounding area and give an all clear.

Simon had decided that his best weapon under the circumstances was sheer audacity. He did not hesitate as he approached the nose of the van, but bore down on it at a dead run. Smoke still hung in the air, but he could see clearly. So could the guards, no doubt, but he hoped to take them completely by surprise. There was nobody near the van, though flashlights were approaching around the side of Hermetico's dome. Someone called out.

"Look! Over there!"

The Saint was already at the door of the van. He flung it open and leaped into the driver's seat as the shouting increased.

"There's one of them!"

"Stop him! Shoot if he won't stop!"

Simon's fingers gratefully closed on the ignition key. The engine chugged unenthusiastically and failed to start. He tried again. The three or four seconds that passed seemed as large and heavy as the columns of Stonehenge. Simon braced the tommy gun against the seat and aimed it into the air through the window.

The men near the building were running towards him, shouting.

"Stop! Come out of there or we'll shoot!"

With one hand he fired his gun harmlessly at the sky as the van's engine at last rumbled to life. The men who had been racing towards him reversed direction and raced back for cover, and there was answering fire from up in the dome. But by then the van had jumped forward and was disappearing into the trees.

Simon kept his head low, and within seconds he was out of danger of being hit by the fire from behind. A large number of very solid trees were acting as his rearguard. He drove around Warlock's police car. Shortly he bounced out into the open field and headed in the direction of the hole in the fence. It was just three o'clock when he finally reached it. He might still get to Amity in time.

He swung out onto the paved road and started back towards Warlock's house by the same route the group had followed on the way to Hermetico. There were much faster roads in the vicinity, but they would be thick with police cars by now, and even on a perfectly normal night the sight of a black van riddled with bullet holes would have been enough to arouse a law officer's interest and cause fatal delays.

So Simon had to go through the agonizing process of travelling winding country lanes at twenty miles an hour when he urgently wanted and needed to be travelling at seventy. Then the process became even more agonizing. About two miles from Hermetico he caught up with a creeping Fiat with a large "L" on its rear bumper. The road was too narrow to allow Simon's van to pass even that minute vehicle, whose driver was apparently not only learner, as his "L" testified, but also an arthritic octogenarian trying very hard to disguise the fact that he was purblind drunk.

Simon tried leaning on his horn, which only stirred the aged pilot of the Fiat to greater excesses of caution. By now the car and the van were moving a scant ten miles an hour . . . and they continued at that pace for five minutes. At last the Saint saw an opening and pushed his way past to the sound of indignant beeps from the Fiat. He then had to steer the van through a series of bends so sharp that having passed the other car proved to have done him almost no good at all.

It was quarter past three and he was not halfway to Warlock's estate. He came at last onto a straight stretch, gathered speed, and swept around a broad curve, only to come face to face with two hundred sheep. The sheep were on a nocturnal stroll of obscure motivation which required that they cross the road en masse in order to get from one identical field to another. Simon tried to push his way through them without killing any, and soon was awash in a sea of angry baas. It was like riding a wave of sheep. For a while it seemed there were sheep in every direction as far as the eye could see. To run over them would soon have either capsized the van or brought it to a halt. There was nothing to do but press on with grimly slow persistence.

When Simon finally broke out of the mass of sheep and got up to speed again it was twenty-five minutes after three. There were no more delays, but even so he was doomed to be late. The hands of his watch indicated three-thirty when he was still a mile from Warlock's house. He swerved around the last bend in the road and tore through the newly repaired gate of Warlock's grounds without slowing down. Ignoring the driveway, he steered a direct path across the lawn to the front door and all but drove up the steps. A short blast from the tommy gun opened the locked door. He kicked it open and ran across the big reception room to the planning room, and then down the stairs to the cellar. To his horror, he could smell something like electricity in the air, then a high-pitched whine and hiss. He burst into the laboratory with his gun ready.

Amity Little turned from the control panel by the wall, where she had been standing adjusting some knobs.

"Oh, Simon!" she beamed, as if she were welcoming him to a cocktail party. "I'm so glad to see you!"

The whine from the electronic equipment dwindled to silence. The Saint's powers of speech dwindled into the same state. He could only stare. Amity came towards him.

"And I was so glad to hear you'd messed things up for Warlock. I knew you would, of course." She looked at him, pretending to be puzzled. "Aren't you glad to see me?"

"Yes," Simon managed. He pointed numbly to some ash on the metal slab to which Amity had been clamped when he left. "Is that . . ."

Amity frowned, then burst into laughter.

"Galaxy? Oh, no. I just used her sweater to try the thing out on. There she is."

Simon looked. Galaxy Rose, looking as voluptuous as ever in spite of mussed hair, a gag in her mouth, and ropes binding her ankles and wrists, was sitting in the corner.

She said "Mump, mump," and glared.

"I've been wanting to shut her up ever since we got here," Amity said. "And I've been wanting to do this, too—right in front of her." She had come up to Simon now, and she put her arms around his neck. "Well?" she murmured. "Aren't you going to thank me for writing you into such lovely adventures?"

He kissed her somewhat hastily.

"And for all the loot we're going to collect from Warlock's safe before the police get here?" she persisted.

He kissed her again, thinking that to thank her properly just for being herself would take considerably more than that.

"But please," said the Saint, with almost frantic restraint, "how did you get off that table?"

Her dazzlingly ingenuous smile would have been absolute justification for homicide.

"Oh, that," she said carelessly. "Well, to find that out, I'm afraid you'll just have to buy my next book."

PUBLICATION

HISTORY

As already mentioned this novel was based on the two-part episode of the same name from *The Saint*, which starred Roger Moore; part one first aired on Sunday, 8 December 1968, and part two first aired on Sunday, 15 December 1968. The script was written by longtime favorite John Kruse with some minor adjustments by script editor Harry Junkin. Charteris loved the script, saying that "*The Fiction Makers* fulfils all the promise of the synopsis, and the dialogue has a crisp sparkle which has all too often been lacking in other scripts. It's true that I still somewhat prefer the treatment of the ending which I suggested. But it is simply a splendid job. I hope there will be a lot more scripts like this." But Kruse was unhappy with the final production: "I was a little disappointed at the way it was filmed. I felt they made it too jokey. The Americans would have played the heavies straight while they were trying to be funny—sort of buffoonery—and that took all the tension out of it and spoiled it . . . *The Fiction Makers* was composed in the way that I most like to compose a story. I had two ideas—nothing whatsoever to do with each other—both of which I very much liked, and suddenly I saw a way to put them together. When that happens you have a very firm basis for a story."[1]

The book was first published in 1968 by the Doubleday Crime Club, with a UK edition appearing on 8 September 1969.

Rather uniquely for the adventures of the Saint, the only foreign translation for this novel was in Turkey, where Gelişim Yayinlari published a paperback edition under the title of *Gerçekleşen düşler* in 1984; the cover for this book featured a stock photo of C-3PO, the gold coloured robot from *Star Wars*. No, we don't know why either.

---

1   Both quotes from *The Saint on TV*, Ian Dickerson (Hirst Publishing, 2011)

ABOUT THE AUTHOR

I'm mad enough to believe in romance. And I'm sick and tired of this age—tired of the miserable little mildewed things that people rucked their brains about, and wrote books about, and called life. I wanted something more elementary and honest—battle, murder, sudden death, with plenty of good beer and damsels in distress, and a complete callousness about blipping the ungodly over the beezer. It mayn't be life as we know it, but it ought to be.

—*Leslie Charteris in a 1935 BBC radio interview*

Leslie Charteris was born Leslie Charles Bowyer-Yin in Singapore on 12 May 1907.

He was the son of a Chinese doctor and his English wife, who'd met in London a few years earlier. Young Leslie found friends hard to come by in colonial Singapore. The English children had been told not to play with Eurasians, and the Chinese children had been told not to play with Europeans. Leslie was caught in between and took refuge in reading.

"I read a great many good books and enjoyed them because nobody had told me that they were classics. I also read a great many bad books which nobody told me not to read . . . I read a great many popular scientific articles and acquired from them an astonishing amount of general knowledge before I discovered that this acquisition was supposed to be a chore."[1]

One of his favourite things to read was a magazine called *Chums*. "The Best and Brightest Paper for Boys" (if you believe the adverts) was a monthly paper full of swashbuckling adventure stories aimed at boys, encouraging them to be honourable and moral and perhaps even "upright citizens with furled umbrellas."[2] Undoubtedly these types of stories would influence his later work.

When his parents split up shortly after the end of World War I, Charteris accompanied his mother and brother back to England, where he was sent to Rossall School in Fleetwood, Lancashire. Rossall was then a very stereotypical English public school, and it struggled to cope with this multilingual mixed-race boy just into his teens who'd already seen more of the world than many of his peers would see in their lifetimes. He was an outsider.

He left Rossall in 1924. Keen to pursue a creative career, he decided to study art in Paris—after all, that was where the great artists went— but soon found that the life of a literally starving artist didn't appeal. He continued writing, firing off speculative stories to magazines, and it was the sale of a short story to *Windsor Magazine* that saved him from penury.

He returned to London in 1925, as his parents—particularly his father—wanted him to become a lawyer, and he was sent to study law at Cambridge University. In the mid-1920s, Cambridge was full of Bright Young Things—aristocrats and bohemians somewhat typified in the Evelyn Waugh novel *Vile Bodies*—and again the mixed-race Bowyer-Yin found that he didn't fit in. He was an outsider who preferred to make his own way in the world and wasn't one of the privileged upper class. It didn't help that he found his studies boring and decided it was more fun contemplating ways to circumvent the law. This inspired him to write a novel, and when publishers Ward Lock & Co. offered him a three-book deal on the strength of it, he abandoned his studies to pursue a writing career.

When his father learnt of this, he was not impressed, as he considered writers to be "rogues and vagabonds." Charteris would later recall that "I wanted to be a writer, he wanted me to become a lawyer. I was stubborn, he said I would end up in the gutter. So I left home. Later on, when I had a little success, we were reconciled by letter, but I never saw him again."[3]

X Esquire, his first novel, appeared in April 1927. The lead character, X Esquire, is a mysterious hero, hunting down and killing the businessmen trying to wipe out Britain by distributing quantities of free poisoned cigarettes. His second novel, *The White Rider*, was published the following spring, and in one memorable scene shows the hero chasing after his damsel in distress, only for him to overtake the villains, leap into their car . . . and promptly faint.

These two plot highlights may go some way to explaining Charteris's comment on *Meet—the Tiger!*, published in September 1928, that "it was only the third book I'd written, and the best, I would say, for it was that the first two were even worse."[4]

Twenty-one-year-old authors are naturally self-critical. Despite reasonably good reviews, the Saint didn't set the world on fire, and Charteris moved on to a new hero for his next book. This was *The Bandit*, an adventure story featuring Ramon Francisco De Castilla y Espronceda Manrique, published in the summer of 1929 after its serialisation in the *Empire News*, a now long-forgotten Sunday newspaper. But sales of *The Bandit* were less than impressive, and Charteris began to question his choice of career. It was all very well writing—but if nobody wants to read what you write, what's the point?

"I had to succeed, because before me loomed the only alternative, the dreadful penalty of failure . . . the routine office hours, the five-day week . . . the lethal assimilation into the ranks of honest, hard-working, conformist, God-fearing pillars of the community."[5]

However his fortunes—and the Saint's—were about to change. In late 1928, Leslie had met Monty Haydon, a London-based editor who was looking for writers to pen stories for his new paper, *The Thriller*— "The Paper with a Thousand Thrills." Charteris later recalled that "he said he was starting a new magazine, had read one of my books and would like some stories from me. I couldn't have been more grateful, both from the point of view of vanity and finance!"[6]

The paper launched in early 1929, and Leslie's first work, "The Story of a Dead Man," featuring Jimmy Traill, appeared in issue 4 (published on 2 March 1929). That was followed just over a month later with "The Secret of Beacon Inn," starring Rameses "Pip" Smith. At the same time, Leslie finished writing another non-Saint novel, *Daredevil*, which would be published in late 1929. Storm Arden was the hero; more notably, the book saw the first introduction of a Scotland Yard inspector by the name of Claud Eustace Teal.

The Saint returned in the thirteenth issue of *The Thriller*. The byline proclaimed that the tale was "A Thrilling Complete Story of the Underworld"; the title was "The Five Kings," and it actually featured Four Kings and a Joker. Simon Templar, of course, was the Joker.

Charteris spent the rest of 1929 telling the adventures of the Five Kings in five subsequent *The Thriller* stories. "It was very hard work, for the pay was lousy, but Monty Haydon was a brilliant and stimulating editor, full of ideas. While he didn't actually help shape the Saint as a character, he did suggest story lines. He would take me out to lunch and say, 'What are you going to write about next?' I'd often say I was damned if I knew. And Monty would say, 'Well, I was reading something the other day . . .' He had a fund of ideas and we would talk them over, and then I would go away and write a story. He was a great creative editor."[7]

Charteris would have one more attempt at writing about a hero other than Simon Templar, in three novelettes published in *The Thriller* in early 1930, but he swiftly returned to the Saint. This was partly due to his self-confessed laziness—he wanted to write more stories for *The Thriller* and other magazines, and creating a new hero for every story was hard work—but mainly due to feedback from Monty Haydon. It seemed people wanted to read more adventures of the Saint . . .

Charteris would contribute over forty stories to *The Thriller* throughout the 1930s. Shortly after their debut, he persuaded publisher Hodder & Stoughton that if he collected some of these stories and rewrote them a little, they could publish them as a Saint book. *Enter the Saint* was first published in August 1930, and the reaction was good enough for the publishers to bring out another collection. And another . . .

Of the twenty Saint books published in the 1930s, almost all have their origins in those magazine stories.

Why was the Saint so popular throughout the decade? Aside from the charm and ability of Charteris's storytelling, the stories, particularly those published in the first half of the '30s, are full of energy and joie de vivre. With economic depression rampant throughout the period, the public at large seemed to want some escapism.

And Simon Templar's appeal was wide-ranging: he wasn't an upper-class hero like so many of the period. With no obvious background and no attachment to the Old School Tie, no friends in high places who could provide a get-out-of-jail-free card, the Saint was uniquely classless. Not unlike his creator.

Throughout Leslie's formative years, his heritage had been an issue. In his early days in Singapore, during his time at school, at Cambridge University or even just in everyday life, he couldn't avoid the fact that for many people his mixed parentage was a problem. He would later tell a story of how he was chased up the road by a stick-waving typical

English gent who took offence to his daughter being escorted around town by a foreigner.

Like the Saint, he was an outsider. And although he had spent a significant portion of his formative years in England, he couldn't settle.

As a young boy he had read of an America "peopled largely by Indians, and characters in fringed buckskin jackets who fought nobly against them. I spent a great deal of time day-dreaming about a visit to this prodigious and exciting country."[8]

It was time to realise this wish. Charteris and his first wife, Pauline, whom he'd met in London when they were both teenagers and married in 1931, set sail for the States in late 1932; the Saint had already made his debut in America courtesy of the publisher Doubleday. Charteris and his wife found a New York still experiencing the tail end of Prohibition, and times were tough at first. Despite sales to *The American Magazine* and others, it wasn't until a chance meeting with writer turned Hollywood executive Bartlett McCormack in their favourite speakeasy that Charteris's career stepped up a gear.

Soon Charteris was in Hollywood, working on what would become the 1933 movie *Midnight Club*. However, Hollywood's treatment of writers wasn't to Charteris's taste, and he began to yearn for home. Within a few months, he returned to the UK and began writing more Saint stories for Monty Haydon and Bill McElroy.

He also rewrote a story he'd sketched out whilst in the States, a version of which had been published in *The American Magazine* in September 1934. This new novel, *The Saint in New York*, published in 1935, was a significant advance for the Saint and Leslie Charteris. Gone were the high jinks and the badinage. The youthful exuberance evident in the Saint's early adventures had evolved into something a little darker, a little more hard-boiled. It was the next stage in development for the author and his creation, and readers loved it. It became a bestseller on both sides of the Atlantic.

Having spent his formative years in places as far apart as Singapore and England, with substantial travel in between, it should be no surprise that Leslie had a serious case of wanderlust. With a bestseller under his belt, he now had the means to see more of the world.

Nineteen thirty-six found him in Tenerife, researching another Saint adventure alongside translating the biography of Juan Belmonte, a well-known Spanish matador. Estranged for several months, Leslie and Pauline divorced in 1937. The following year, Leslie married an American, Barbara Meyer, who'd accompanied him to Tenerife. In early 1938, Charteris and his new bride set off in a trailer of his own design and spent eighteen months travelling round America and Canada.

The Saint in New York had reminded Hollywood of Charteris's talents, and film rights to the novel were sold prior to publication in 1935. Although the proposed 1935 film production was rejected by the Hays Office for its violent content, RKO's eventual 1938 production persuaded Charteris to try his luck once more in Hollywood.

New opportunities had opened up, and throughout the 1940s the Saint appeared not only in books and movies but in a newspaper strip, a comic-book series, and on radio.

Anyone wishing to adapt the character in any medium found a stern taskmaster in Charteris. He was never completely satisfied, nor was he shy of showing his displeasure. He did, however, ensure that copyright in any Saint adventure belonged to him, even if scripted by another writer—a contractual obligation that he was to insist on throughout his career.

Charteris was soon spread thin, overseeing movies, comics, newspapers, and radio versions of his creation, and this, along with his self-proclaimed laziness, meant that Saint books were becoming fewer and further between. However, he still enjoyed his creation: in 1941 he indulged himself in a spot of fun by playing the Saint—complete with monocle and moustache—in a photo story in *Life* magazine.

In July 1944, he started collaborating under a pseudonym on Sherlock Holmes radio scripts, subsequently writing more adventures for Holmes than Conan Doyle. Not all his ventures were successful—a screenplay he was hired to write for Deanna Durbin, "Lady on a Train," took him a year and ultimately bore little resemblance to the finished film. In the mid-1940s, Charteris successfully sued RKO Pictures for unfair competition after they launched a new series of films starring George Sanders as a debonair crime fighter known as the Falcon. But he kept faith with his original character, and the Saint novels continued to adapt to the times. The transatlantic Saint evolved into something of a private operator, working for the mysterious Hamilton and becoming, not unlike his creator, a world traveller, finding that adventure would seek him out.

"I have never been able to see why a fictional character should not grow up, mature, and develop, the same as anyone else. The same, if you like, as his biographer. The only adequate reason is that—so far as I know—no other fictional character in modern times has survived a sufficient number of years for these changes to be clearly observable. I must confess that a lot of my own selfish pleasure in the Saint has been in watching him grow up."[9]

Charteris maintained his love of travel and was soon to be found sailing round the West Indies with his good friend Gregory Peck. His forays abroad gave him even more material, and he began to write true-crime articles, as well as an occasional column in *Gourmet* magazine.

By the early '50s, Charteris himself was feeling strained. He'd divorced his second wife in 1943 and got together with a New York radio and nightclub singer called Betty Bryant Borst, whom he married in late 1943. That relationship had fallen apart acrimoniously towards the end of the decade, and he roamed the globe restlessly, rarely in one place for longer than a couple of months. He continued to maintain a firm grip on the exploitation of the Saint in various media but was writing little himself. The Saint had become an industry, and Charteris couldn't keep up. He began thinking seriously about an early retirement.

Then in 1951 he met a young actress called Audrey Long when they became next-door neighbours in Hollywood. Within a year they had married, a union that was to last the rest of Leslie's life.

He attacked life with a new vitality. They travelled—Nassau was a favoured escape spot—and he wrote. He struck an agreement with *The New York Herald Tribune* for a Saint comic strip, which would appear daily and be written by Charteris himself. The strip ran for thirteen years, with Charteris sending in his handwritten story lines from wherever he happened to be, relying on mail services around the world to continue the Saint's adventures. New Saint books began to appear, and Charteris reached a height of productivity not seen since his days as a struggling author trying to establish himself. As Leslie and Audrey travelled, so did the Saint, visiting locations just after his creator had been there.

By 1953 the Saint had already enjoyed twenty-five years of success, and *The Saint Detective Magazine* was launched. Charteris had become adept at exploiting his creation to the full, mixing new stories with repackaged older stories, sometimes rewritten, sometimes mixed up in "new" anthologies, sometimes adapted from radio scripts previously written by other writers.

Charteris had been approached several times over the years for television rights in the Saint and had expended much time and effort during the 1950s trying to get the Saint on TV, even going so far as to write sample scripts himself, but it wasn't to be. He finally agreed a deal in autumn 1961 with English film producers Robert S. Baker and Monty Berman. The first episode of *The Saint* television series, starring Roger Moore, went into production in June 1962. The series was an immediate success, though Charteris himself had his reservations. It reached second place in the ratings, but he commented that "in that distinction it was topped by wrestling, which only suggested to me that the competition may not have been so hot; but producers are generally cast in a less modest mould." He resented the implication that the TV series had finally made a success of the Saint after twenty-five years of literary obscurity.

As long as the series lasted, Charteris was not shy about voicing his criticisms both in public and in a constant stream of memos to the producers. "Regular followers of the Saint saga . . . must have noticed that I am almost incapable of simply writing a story and shutting up."[10] Nor was he shy about exploiting this new market by agreeing to a series of tie-in novelisations ghosted by other writers, which he would then rewrite before publication.

Charteris mellowed as the series developed and found elements to praise too. He developed a close friendship with producer Robert S. Baker, which would last until Charteris's death.

In the early '60s, on one of their frequent trips to England, Leslie and Audrey bought a house in Surrey, which became their permanent base. He explored the possibility of a Saint musical and began writing some of it himself.

Charteris no longer needed to work. Now in his sixties, he supervised the Saint from a distance whilst continuing to travel and indulge himself. He and Audrey made seasonal excursions to Ireland and the south of France, where they had residences. He began to write poetry and devised a new universal sign language, Paleneo, based on notes and symbols he used in his diaries. Once Paleneo was released, he decided enough was enough and announced, again, his retirement. This time he meant it.

The Saint continued regardless—there was a long-running Swedish comic strip, and new novels with other writers doing the bulk of the work were complemented in the 1970s with Bob Baker's revival of the TV series, *Return of the Saint.*

Ill-health began to take its toll. By the early 1980s, although he continued a healthy correspondence with the outside world, Charteris felt unable to keep up with the collaborative Saint books and pulled the plug on them.

To entertain himself, Leslie took to "trying to beat the bookies in predicting the relative speed of horses," a hobby which resulted in several of his local betting shops refusing to take "predictions" from him, as he was too successful for their liking.

He still received requests to publish his work abroad but had become completely cynical about further attempts to revive the Saint. A new Saint magazine only lasted three issues, and two TV productions—*The Saint in Manhattan*, with Tom Selleck look-alike Andrew Clarke, and *The Saint*, with Simon Dutton—left him bitterly disappointed. "I fully expect this series to lay eggs everywhere . . . the only satisfaction I have is in looking at my bank balance."[11]

In the early 1990s, Hollywood producers Robert Evans and William J. Macdonald approached him and made a deal for the Saint to return to cinema screens. Charteris still took great care of the Saint's reputation and wrote an outline entitled *The Return of the Saint* in which an older Saint would meet the son he didn't know he had.

Much of his time in his last few years was taken up with the movie. Several scripts were submitted to him—each moving further and further away from his original concept—but the screenwriter from 1940s Hollywood was thoroughly disheartened by the Hollywood of the '90s: "There is still no plot, no real story, no characterisations, no personal interaction, nothing but endless frantic violence . . ." Besides, with producer Bill Macdonald hitting the headlines for the most un-Saintly reasons, he was to add, "How can Bill Macdonald concentrate on my Saint movie when he has Sharon Stone in his bed?"

The Crime Writers' Association of Great Britain presented Leslie with a Lifetime Achievement award in 1992 in a special ceremony at the

House of Lords. Never one for associations and awards, and although visibly unwell, Leslie accepted the award with grace and humour ("I am now only waiting to be carbon-dated," he joked). He suffered a slight stroke in his final weeks, which did not prevent him from dining out locally with family and friends, before he finally passed away at the age of 85 on 15 April 1993.

His death severed one of the final links with the classic thriller genre of the 1930s and 1940s, but he left behind a legacy of nearly one hundred books, countless short stories, and TV, film, radio, and comic-strip adaptations of his work which will endure for generations to come.

> *I was always sure that there was a solid place in escape literature for a rambunctious adventurer such as I dreamed up in my youth, who really believed in the old-fashioned romantic ideals and was prepared to lay everything on the line to bring them to life. A joyous exuberance that could not find its fulfilment in pinball machines and pot. I had what may now seem a mad desire to spread the belief that there were worse, and wickeder, nut cases than Don Quixote.*
>
> *Even now, half a century later, when I should be old enough to know better, I still cling to that belief. That there will always be a public for the old-style hero, who had a clear idea of justice, and a more than technical approach to love, and the ability to have some fun with his crusades.*[12]

---

1 *A Letter from the Saint*, 30 August 1946
2 "The Last Word," *The First Saint Omnibus*, Doubleday Crime Club, 1939
3 *The Straits Times*, 29 June 1958, page 9

4 Introduction by Charteris to the September 1980 paperback reprint of *Meet—the Tiger!* (Charter), the last ever print edition.

5 *The Saint: A Complete History*, by Burl Barer (McFarland, 1993)

6 PR material from the 1970s series *Return of the Saint*

7 From "Return of the Saint: Comprehensive Information" issued to help publicise the 1970s TV show

8 *A Letter from the Saint*, 26 July 1946

9 Introduction to "The Million Pound Day," in *The First Saint Omnibus*

10 *A Letter from the Saint*, 12 April 1946

11 Letter from LC to sometime Saint collaborator Peter Bloxsom, 2 August 1989

12 Introduction by Charteris to the September 1980 paperback reprint of *Meet—the Tiger!* (Charter).

WATCH FOR THE SIGN
OF THE SAINT!

THE SAINT CLUB

*And so, my friends, dear bookworms, most noble fellow
drinkers, frustrated burglars, affronted policemen, upright
citizens with furled umbrellas and secret buccaneering
dreams that seems to be very nearly all for now. It has been
nice having you with us, and we hope you will come again,
not once, but many times.*

*Only because of our great love for you, we would like
to take this parting opportunity of mentioning one small
matter which we have very much at heart . . .*

—Leslie Charteris, The First Saint Omnibus *(1939)*

Leslie Charteris founded The Saint Club in 1936 with the aim of providing a constructive fanbase for Saint devotees. Before the War, it donated profits to a London hospital where, for several years, a Saint ward was maintained. With the nationalisation of hospitals, profits were, for many years, donated to the Arbour Youth Centre in Stepney, London.

In the twenty-first century, we've carried on this tradition but have also donated to the Red Cross and a number of different children's charities.

The club acts as a focal point for anyone interested in the adventures of Leslie Charteris and the work of Simon Templar, and offers merchandise that includes DVDs of the old TV series and various Saint-related publications, through to its own exclusive range of notepaper, pin badges, and polo shirts. All profits are donated to charity. The club also maintains two popular websites and supports many more Saint-related sites.

After Leslie Charteris's death, the club recruited three new vice-presidents—Roger Moore, Ian Ogilvy, and Simon Dutton have all pledged their support, whilst Audrey and Patricia Charteris have been retained as Saints-in-Chief. But some things do not change, for the back of the membership card still mischievously proclaims that . . .

> *The bearer of this card is probably a person of hideous*
> *antecedents and low moral character, and upon*
> *apprehension for any cause should be immediately released*
> *in order to save other prisoners from contamination.*

To join . . .

Membership costs £3.50 (or US$7) per year, or £30 (US$60) for life. Find us online at www.lesliecharteris.com for full details.

Made in the USA
Coppell, TX
04 August 2025

52644991R00146